apocalypse (n.)

also by Amy Longworth

Nothing, yet.

apocalypse (n.)

a true story, for all intents and purposes

Amy Longworth

Copyright © 2020 Amy Longworth

All rights reserved.

ISBN-13: 978-0-578-67674-6

Cover artwork by Julia Clementson

www.juliaclementson.com

to the Homeless Encampment, for taking in a stray British lady.
thank you for your support.

They came largely to get away - that most simple of motives. To get away. Away from what? In the long run, away from themselves. Away from everything. That's why most people have come to America, and do still come. To get away from everything they are and have been.

DH Lawrence, "Studies in Classic American Literature"

prologue

brian

11/30/19

We had to let him go, love. We had to let him go.

As he spoke, I saw the scene in my grandparents' dining room exactly as it was. It was as it had always been.

I was eight thousand miles away, and I was sitting on a slab of pavement outside work. Work was in Phoenix, Arizona - and it was not in Oxfordshire, England.

But - I was there anyway. In England, or At Home, or whatever we want to call it. Even from so far away, I could see them. The scene was laid out before my eyes, because it hadn't changed.

Nan was standing at an angle in the kitchen, and Dad was watching her, a rough cheek pressed against the landline, and Sam was on the matt by the back door. Dad's T-shirt was mucky with age, and his brow was furrowed, and he was ruddy-faced and bristly, and his mind was pottering through the things at hand - me, and the tea, and Grandad's death.

Dad long ago mastered the art of tea-time-timing and talking, so his position suited him perfectly. The landline is in the corner of my grandparents' dining room, above the wooden cupboard stuffed with all the papers and trinkets that I'd pulled out and pored over, over and over, as a child. The walls are shantily wallpapered with corkboard, and on top of the cork there's an odd combination of wartime poster prints and collie-dog photos and all of the Christmas cards that Nick and Bryn sent back from America every Christmas. And none of it is in chronological order.

And the dining room is small enough that the coil of the line stretches easily to the bench if you want to have a seat while you talk. From there, the vantage of the galley kitchen is prime. It's convenient, because it means that stovetop veg can be presided over when the phone goes and you end up having a natter with whoever it is that's ringing.

In this case the nattering was with me, The Eldest Grandchild, and I was ringing because I was a very long way away, desperate to be home again, because Grandad was dead.

/

It always takes me aback, a little, when people ask if I'm close with my grandparents. I'm never sure how to do justice to the question - to me, my grandparents are, quite simply, part of the furniture of my childhood.

It was as it was. It was me, and Meg, and Emily, and Luke, and we were the grandkids. Above us, there was Dad and Auntie Ann and Uncle Ian, and they were the kids. And Nan and Grandad were just - Nan and Grandad. Brian and Kay.

To my mind, anyone who knew them as Brian and Kay were Old People, like the other Old People in the village who drifted together for things like Senior Cits' Coffee Morning, and Church, and The Village Fete.

I never thought of Nan and Grandad the same way as I thought about other Old People, because other Old People smelled fusty and moved slowly and were very, very boring. Nan and Grandad, on the contrary, were not boring. Nan and Grandad were robust and upright, outdoorsy, always moving, always finding something to do Around The House or Around The Village or On The Weekends.

They lived at 4 The Croft, which also had a sign on it marking it *Wheal Porth*, even though no-one ever called it that, and no-one was even sure what it meant.

Either way, their house was the cornerstone of the good parts of our childhoods.

Nan and Grandad were who we went to on the weekends and for the summers and for the Christmases. When we arrived, Nan would holler a genial *hell-ohhh*, and kiss us wetly after the dog did, and Grandad would follow with a gruffer greeting, no affectionate gestures necessary. He had the unparalleled ability to make a *hello* sound like a retort.

We'd invariably all park up at the table, and the kettle would go on, and tea would be administered to those who wanted it. The table was the center of their little universe, and it never aged underneath all the scratches and spillages, the baking sessions and the weight of our feasts. Time spent at it never got old, either. A million breakfasts and lunches and teas were had at the table, just how a million mornings and afternoons were spent outside the house entirely, striding alongside some canal or across some forest or through acres of sodden fields. I went over a million G2's at the table, snaffled from Grandad's daily Guardian, and the dog always lapped up a million crumbs after a good meal overhead. At the table, Grandad heard a million Penguin-wrapper jokes that he didn't want to hear, and we ate through a million main courses with a million over-boiled vegetables, anticipating a million toffee yogurts afterward. Or cakes, if we'd been lucky and it was a baking day.

At the table, we gave Dad our leftovers, we rolled out gingerbread men, we mashed jelly diamonds into wet icing, we labored over jigsaws, we left Whoopee cushions under suspecting bottoms, we snickered and we yakked and we sulked - and Grandad presided over all of it, a wry patriarch to his frenetic brood. As a collective, we became known as The Rabble. It was probably Grandad who coined the term.

And then, as we grew up, we started to call Grandad by his real name. Brian. Brian Longworth.

Brian Longworth was bespectacled, clean shaven, and methodical. He clad himself in Rohan trousers and Rohan shirts and pulled-up socks and sensible shoes, and this fact never changed. He consumed his coffee with evaporated milk at eleven o'clock, on the dot, and he drank ginger ale and Pepsi Max at lunchtime, and he always ate everything on his plate at every mealtime. This also never changed. He armed himself with a pen, a Swiss army knife, and a mental pocketbook of quips to be trotted out in a low stage-whisper, given the appropriate circumstance - a favorite was always an immaculately-timed, ever-infuriating Nat King Cole lyric - *smile, though your heart is breaking.* This also never changed. His face was punctuated with a scowl, a dimple on his chin, and a thick pair of glasses. This most certainly never changed. This was a fact of his existence.

As a Rabble, we were inclined to think of Brian a grouch, a curmudgeon, a stoic with a face that didn't budge when we descended into hysterics when the F-word - that is, *fart* - was mentioned. As birthdays and school years ticked by, however, the gradual warming was inevitable. Brian had always talked, but we started to listen, and - ever the man to appreciate an eager ear to talk at - he started to take us seriously. Or at least grow fond of the extra ears.

And despite his meticulously chiselled sensibilities, and his distaste for all manner of things - to include Tories and Americans, Church and Senior Citizens - it became abundantly clear to me, in my teenage years, that Brian was one of the kindest men I'll ever know. I can say with conviction that I have witnessed some deeply beautiful marriages, and his marriage to my Nan - to Kay, who, to this day, is a scurrying nymph of a woman - is the very best of them all. The worst words I ever heard cross his lips towards her was a textbook, jesting quip of his - *my love for you is lasting/like snow on the desert sand.*

(I never got the chance to show him the photos, taken from my own front door, that snow does, in fact, settle in the desert).

His kindness manifested itself in so many small, gorgeous ways. His kindness was the glee of a wartime child, aged seventy-or-eighty-something, at the prospect of jam *and* butter, at the same time, on the same slice of bread. His kindness was in the refusal to let go of that little triumph, to let it slide while his grandchildren wolfed down luxuries he never had - that didn't exist - when he was the dark-haired, surly-looking kid I know he was. His kindness was there in his unfettered joy for The Museum - that is, his shed, which was a wooden outhouse filled with miniature trains and traction engines and WWII-era aircraft. His kindness was there in his watchfulness, because - well, Brian was a man who strode ahead of everyone else on our walks because it was the right place for the man who loved his pack.

And then there were the quaint little kindnesses, the little joys of his that he harbored with steady zeal. There was his penchant for thick-cut marmalade, and ginger candy, and - oddly enough - ABBA. "ABBA Gold" was the only CD we could ever all agree upon on our drives to the canals and the forests and the fields that made each of us ardent lovers of the outdoors.

Brian didn't frighten us, or coddle us, or prod at us. Brian sat back and quietly suffered his tornado of grandchildren until we became old enough for us to actually listen to the stories he'd told us a million times. We started hitting the milestones that, in his eyes, were metrics of success - A-level grades, university acceptances, degrees. And he applauded our academic victories with a token, cursory, *Very Good.*

My marriage did not receive the same level of affection. He was, after all, an American. I thought that maybe the fact that my future husband was a Marine might save him, because of the war and all, and - I don't know, I think it earned him a bit more interest than another sort of American might have done. But all the same - it did not save America. Not in Brian's eyes.

So it was a Bit Of A Shame that I had to move there and everything.

When I left for America I wept once. Just once. I wept when I left my grandparents' house, because it might not be the same place when I came back.

And it wasn't.

/

The first time I came home, after America became a Real Place, something was amiss. Grandad was - doddery. He swept through a stop sign on our way to Millet's Farm into oncoming traffic. He walked at a marked angle. He was slower, and while he'd always been repetitive - a trait of his that lay somewhere between charming and tedious - he was more repetitious than ever.

I left, of course. I went back to America, the land of the Trumps and the relentless weather. And between visits - almost two years of his waning life, and my own increasingly bizarre one - he was diagnosed with dementia. After a particularly bad fall it was appropriate to admit him to a nursing home. I still find it difficult to marry that phrase - *a bad fall* - with the sturdy, scathing man I'd always known. It better fits the other OAPs that Brian sniffed at.

Nevertheless, the nursing home it was. Off he went, off to the nursing home, asking constantly when it was that he was Going Home.

The next - and last - time I saw Brian was in the square, linoleummed setting of that nursing home, St. Katherine's Care Home. The Home was as unhomely as a place could possibly be. It was bleached and it was barren and it was squeaky. There was no corkboard or collie-dogs or Christmas cards - just corridors, lots of corridors, and very squeaky floors.

Dad led us into a room that was supposed to be the living room, and Brian was sitting in a straight-backed pink chair in the corner, and the chair didn't move. He didn't move, either. He was just slack. Slack and thin-skinned.

My breath caught the moment I saw him. Grandad - Brian, Grandad, my clean, quippy grandad - was an ember. He looked like a vagrant version of someone who might have been him if you squinted. He didn't move. And he - he was scruffy.

No-one had taken the time to shave him that morning.
It was the first time I'd ever seen him unshaven.

We had brought him some peanut brittle, and he expressed what might have passed as an exclamation at the gift. He ate it then and there, using his slipper as a plate from which he ate in the same systematic manner he'd always eaten with.

I remember that cloying, clinical excuse for a living room like it was yesterday. The clock was stuck at ten to seven.

/

When he passed, Dad received the phone call at two o'clock in the morning. He had *had a few moments* with Grandad the next day. I'm not sure what that looked like.

This Christmas, I'm coming home to an England without Grandad. I'm not sure what that looks like, either. It's been six years since I was at home - truly at home - at Christmastime. I don't know how it will feel to have the requisite Boxing Day Walk without Grandad pioneering the way.

/

Dad said something else while we were on the phone that day, between his diligent veg-watch and my own inane nattering. The interesting thing about Grandad, he said, was that while his brain started to eat away at itself, his health was otherwise fantastic. His heart, Dad remarked, was as healthy as it had ever been.

There's a comfort in knowing that the man who, in myriad ways, gave a steady pulse to each of our lives, was still ticking onwards in a manner uncharacteristic of other men pushing ninety. Maybe it was genetic. Maybe it was all the walking. Maybe it was love.

Whatever it was, I'm glad I got to share as much of my life with Brian Longworth as I did.

When I learned that Grandad had died, I made a decision. I decided to keep his name. I don't know where I picture myself in the future, but I do know that Brian Longworth will always be a part of my identity, now, by name alone.

I'm also not sure when the day of his funeral will be, but I do know that on the day of his funeral, I will walk along the canal here in Phoenix, and I will imagine narrowboats - scores of them - and I will smile, though my heart is breaking.

And I will be Amy Longworth.

/

As opposed to Amy Byrne.

<u>now</u>

3/18/20

Today's date is red, then white, then orange.

That seems like a good starting point.

That also wouldn't make sense to anyone else reading this, other than me. No one else marries the number three with red, or the number one with white, or the number eight with orange.

But I do. And I'm not really sure what to write about at the moment because the world seems to be going up in flames - but I do know that it makes sense to start somewhere familiar.

I like that today's date is all fire colors.

I like that it's raining in Phoenix.

I like that the construction men outside know that they can ask me for coffee or snacks if they need them.

And I like that I have some time away from work for a bit. I like that I have some time to write for a bit. And I like that the plan is to get me back to Twentynine Palms for a bit.

I'd like to say I don't like being stuck in Phoenix and out of work for the time being. But it all makes sense. I came to Phoenix to be Elsewhere, just like how I came to America to be Elsewhere, and now I'm here, square in the middle of Elsewhere, and as it turns out, I'm stuck - and the only way to make it okay is to make it into something beautiful.

And I know I can do that.

I also know the word *apocalypse* is a lot of colors all at once.

So that's roughly the plan here. The rough *course of action*, as Killian would have said. Although - well, I'm not sure courses of action are allowed to be rough.

But this is real life, and it is not the Marine Corps, so I'm saying it anyway.

<u>now</u>

3/18/20

There are two men working on number 28. They make a lot of noise, during the day, but as far as people go, they're really nice. They don't pry. They just try and say nice things to me when I'm outside and we're all in the same space.

Yesterday I was sat outside my apartment and one of them asked me if I had kids, or a husband.

And I said no. It was just me.

I said I had had a husband, but now I didn't have a husband. So - *yeah*, it was just me. *Me and the dog.*

I didn't say that my ex-husband's name is Killian and that he's actually a really great person. And I also didn't say that I'm actually very happy with the way things are right now.

The man said he had kids, a big one and a little one, and he said that the little one was two-and-a-half. He seemed to recommend children. He said it was *lovely*, very lovely, to have children. He didn't give me their names, or talk about their favorite things, but it was very clear that he loved them.

When I left for my walk, I apologized for the dog. I told them his name is Sonny, and I told them that he was going to bark at them, and that I couldn't help it, and that at the end of the day I was very pleased that he was doing his job but I was very sorry about the noise, and - well, normally he's very nice.

Where we came from, I didn't have to worry about this, I said. I neglected to mention that Sonny had grown up in the desert, the proper desert, and that we'd had a lot of space, and that there weren't a lot of people in the desert for him to bark at when he was Being Protective. Which was also his job.

He's just being protective, I said. *I know it's annoying, but it's just what he does.*

Today, I asked if they needed coffee. It was just the two of them, and they were working on four units all by themselves, and I'm not sure where the guy who lives next door to me was, but - well, I was home for once because coronavirus was a thing, and I wasn't sure if I had a job any more, so it made sense to be the person that the construction men could call on if they needed something.

So I told them to knock if they needed anything.

I went out and I did some things and I got some hand sanitizer, and then I came back. And then I smoked a cigarette in my empty parking spot because I didn't want to get under their feet.

When I came back up, I asked again, even though they hadn't knocked. And the one I hadn't talked to yesterday spoke worse English, but he did say a snack would be nice.

I went in and came out and gave him some Clif bars. And he was excited about the fact they were peanut butter Clif bars, so I guess I did something right.

And then I went to the pool with Sonny. I didn't have him on the leash, and he ran off when we were supposed to come back because he heard other dogs barking. I knew he just wanted to be close to them. He just wanted to be nice.

When Sonny ran off, the construction men seemed concerned. They peered over the railings and they pronounced his name wrong and they whistled. And I stood by my door, and I knew their name-calling and their whistling was useless, and I told them he'd be back.

And right on cue, he came right back.

<u>now</u>

3/19/20

Before Sonny, there was Max. Max is the cat I named after we watched "Mad Max" at Candice's house, before we took off and drove to somewhere that looked post-apocalyptic.

Killian had been told he had to go to Twentynine Palms for a bit, and so Twentynine Palms was what we were doing. I didn't know much about Twentynine Palms before we got there, except that it looked like what I imagined Mars looked like, and that we were going to live there for the foreseeable future, and that it was hotter out there than I'd ever thought possible.

Although, if I'm being really honest, I kind of liked the idea of living somewhere that looked like it didn't belong on Earth.

I had been in England, during the moving process. While I was in England, Killian had acquired some cats, and Max was the runt of the litter, and Max didn't really know how to eat, and even Killian knew from the get-go that Max would be mine.

If you'd asked me a few years ago where I'd end up feeling alright, I wouldn't have thought that it would be in the desert with a dog and a cat and an apartment full of pretty things, but - well, it also makes sense that this is how things have ended up.

The three of us moved into this apartment nine-ish months ago, and somehow we made it work.

/

Max started out in life as a stray, by the way. Killian picked him up with his brothers in an abandoned building in Quantico while I was in England, and we decided to keep them, even though I was angry that Mingy might not like them. Alex was Killian's best friend, who had lived with us for a bit in California, and Mingy was Alex's cat, and he'd left her on the east coast, and so we were sort of renting her with a mind to eventually deliver her back to him, but she was the first pet I'd had in America that wasn't a goldfish, so - well, I guess I gave a shit about her wellbeing. And I knew that ol' Minge would not like the kittens.

But Killian insisted that we keep the kittens, so that's what we did.

When I got back from England that summer, he'd moved us out of our apartment the day before I arrived back, so we had to spend the night at Candice's house, and that's where I met Max. Max fitted into my palm, and we weren't sure what to call him, but "Mad Max" was on in the background and we were about to go and live somewhere that looked like the end of the world - so Max it was.

Killian had already named Max's brother after Rick from "Rick and Morty," and - yeah, it was somehow pretty well established that Rick was his cat and Max would be mine.

The next day we started the drive from Stafford, Virginia, to Twentynine Palms, California, with one cat and three kittens. One Mingy and three mewling, shitting kittens. Killian was the driver and I was the cat-wrangler, and we listened to a lot of Hozier and we stayed in whichever motels allowed cats. We segued to Oceanside before we got to Twentynine Palms, and that's where we gave Mingy back to Alex.

We joked a lot about how Mingy looked like Max's mom, because she was also black-and-white. But she also hated Max, so it was good that she had somewhere to go where she'd be unburdened of the unforeseen strays that we attached to ourselves.

For a year or so, it was just us and the cats. I started working at GNC, because I knew I'd go a bit mad if I didn't have work, and I'd walked into GNC and I asked if they were hiring, and Trevor had liked me, and so GNC hired me.

So Killian did Marine Things, and I did GNC Things, and that was that. Us, and work, and the cats.

We called the cats the Shittens, and they grew up pretty much as expected - Rick got loud and fat, and Max was a wimp who just needed to be held a lot. And we were pretty alright that way. Max was mine and Rick was Killian's and that's just how it was. We probably joked about how easy it would be to divvy up the cats if the Hypothetical Divorce happened.

Sonny appeared on a Sunday morning in November when I was getting ready to go to work. One of Killian's Marines shot out a group text asking if anyone wanted a puppy and - well, we hadn't wanted a puppy, but we saw the message and we looked at each other, and we said *I guess we're getting a dog.*

So after I got off work that evening, we got a dog.

We didn't like the name Sonny, but he was used to his name at that point, so we changed the U to an O, and we liked it a bit more after that.

The cats hated Sonny. When I took him outside they'd peer at him through the back door, and when he tried to get near them they would spit and hiss and throw claws.

I didn't really know much about dog ownership, but I'd learnt a bit from my grandparents, and that was that Dogs Need Walks.

So Sonny and I started walking.

It was kind of reckless of me to walk him before he got his shots, but I did it anyway. I guess I figured that if he got the parvovirus that everyone was banging on about, then he'd get sick for a bit and then he'd be okay, and - I don't know, ultimately he was happier being outside with me than he was when he was cooped up indoors. When we kept him inside for too long he would chew things, and when he got enough exercise he was good, so I implemented a strict walking regimen to make him happy. It made me happy, too. I hadn't been all that happy sitting indoors watching TV shows that Killian wanted to watch and I didn't, so having an excuse to go outside was really quite nice.

Our desert walks were always the same. From our house on base, we'd walk along the side of the stucco-coated, jejune neighborhood that I had once been thrilled to live in. We'd go past the gas station, up towards the only paved path from the neighborhood to Mainside. Once on that path, it was mostly just dirt and sand and palm trees and a gas station for tanks. Occasionally, armored vehicles would trundle out in a convoy alongside us and I'd wave at the drivers. Mostly, though, we passed no one. At the right time of day - sunrise, or sunset - it was beautiful. The sky was enormous, and the desert was vast, and my music was whatever I needed it to be, and it was just us. And that was all the comfort I needed.

After Killian deployed, I started letting Sonny sleep on the bed. That worked well for both of us, because I liked having something next to me when I slept. Around that time, the cats started to tolerate Sonny a bit more. I think maybe all of us sleeping in close proximity had something to do with it.

Sonny was the one who was there when Killian was having more fun than me while he was on deployment. Sonny became more than a dog at that point. He stopped being a puppy for a moment as soon as I started crying, and he let me put my arms around him and sob into his fur.

And it was the animals that led to the thing that made me and Killian get divorced.

I had a fever, and I was at work, and Killian was in the field, and so I asked M to go over and let Sonny out so that I could just come home and not worry about walking Sonny. I figured he'd appreciate the time spent in a real house with a dog, instead of sitting around in the barracks.

When I got home there was a bottle of Tullamore Dew on the counter. And Kant.

Fast forward a few hours, and things started to become undone.

/

The divorce documents said -

Each of us also understands that even after a Joint Petition for Summary Dissolution is filed, this entire agreement will be canceled if either of us revokes the dissolution proceeding.

    II. Division of Community Property We divide our community property as follows:

        1. Amy transfers to Killian as Killian's sole and separate property:

            A. Household furnishings located at the 3302B Fuller St residence.
            B. All rights to cash in NFCU savings and checking accounts.
            C. All USMC Thrift Savings Plan (TSP) earned during the marriage.
            D. Killian's jewelry (one diamond engagement ring).
            E. One 2015 Toyota Tacoma
            F. One 2008 Triumph Daytona
            G. One pet cat named "Rick"

        2. Killian transfers to Amy as Amy's sole and separate property:

            A. Household furnishings located at the 3302B Fuller St residence.
            B. One pet dog named "Sonny"
            C. One pet cat named "Max"

Neither of us had a single disagreement about who got what pet. Max had always been mine, and I was the only one who walked

Sonny, and I didn't like Rick's shrieking, so that's just how the dominos fell.

And now I'm in Phoenix. And life doesn't look the way I wanted it to, but my apartment does, and I have two animals that have somehow kept me a bit sane through a time where I was pretty unravelled.

And now the coronavirus is making other people become unravelled, and it's making people need to be close to the people they love, and since all of mine are on another continent, I'm just really fucking grateful that I have a dog and a cat that I can call my own.

I'm leaving them, though, because I have to go back to Twentynine Palms.

All that B had had to say was that he'd had a dog before deployment, and now he's back, and now the dog is not there.

Right now, Friends feels like the closest thing to Family that I've got over here. So - well, now that the world is starting to fall to pieces, I'd rather be in Twentynine Palms with B and his friend Creg than Elsewhere. And Elsewhere is where I'd go if I got stuck in my apartment as the heat starts to rise outside.

So we made a plan to get me back to Twentynine Palms for a bit.

a bit before

3/13/20

I told B I was going for dinner this weekend with the guy we all swooned over at work, and he asked if I was going on Friday and - well, I'd been drinking gin, so I didn't think to ask why he asked about Friday specifically until after I'd opened the message and replied and then slept a bit and thought about it again when I woke up.

And I said - *Why Friday*

And he said he was figuring some things out but he might be in the area on Friday, which meant he was back and it meant he wanted to come and see me as a Real Person now that he was back in America and he was a Real Person again.

It was Friday the 13th. The world was falling to pieces because coronavirus was a thing, and the supermarkets were stripped of ramen and canned goods and toilet paper, and people were harping on about washing their hands, and there were videos of dead people in the street on the Internet. It was raining in Phoenix, and it had been raining on and off for three days, occasionally with an outburst of thunder but mostly just a drum of alien greyness. The day before, I lent my boss my back-up umbrella to keep her a bit drier on her excursion to Fry's, and it turned out that it was the first time in her life that she'd used an umbrella, and something about this fact coupled with The Pandemic and the rain and the sudden stupidity of it all made us laugh, and we couldn't stop laughing even though the world was apparently upside down now.

After work I went to Fry's with the intent to buy the groceries I'd taken from Lauren's, which then turned into me needing to buy a lot of wine, so I went from the average grocery store to the bougie grocery store and ended up buying carrots at the store I shouldn't have needed carrots in. Either way - I got Lauren's La Croix for Lauren's vodka, and I also got a weekend's worth of $3 wine.

So there I was, standing in line with a cart slightly full of brown plastic bags from the store across the street and otherwise full with La Croix and $3 wine and root vegetables because I figured quarantine would be best spent slightly inebriated and my Grandma's soup recipe was cheap and would feed us for weeks - and then me and another lady started talking because we'd set up camp in line, and the line wasn't exactly long, but it was going to take some time because the people ahead of us were buying cartfuls.

The lady's cart was full, too. I noticed the items - organic pretzel bites amongst the pile of organic frozen dinners. Her hair was red, like mine, but she was older. We hummed and huffed over the State of Things for a minute. I just remember all the bottles of good-for-you sunscreen that lined up beside her head when she talked.

I looked back at her cart. Down the aisle. She said her husband had cancer and she was afraid.

He was waiting in the car, she said.

He was one eighty and now he's one forty and he just lost eight pounds of fluid today, she said.

Her eyes welled up.

I asked if she needed a hug. And she did.

So there we were - two strangers hugging amidst the fucking coronavirus chaos. Lentils and popcorn were scarce and everyone wanted toilet paper and pasta and no one wanted to touch another person, but we hugged anyway.

I told her I would help in any way I could.

She said her name was Debbie. She said she'd been married for thirty-one years. She said his name is David. She said he has a neuroendocrine tumor and she said something else about his pancreas. He was waiting in the car and they lived in Litchfield Park which is about thirty minutes away, she said.

I didn't say that they had been married three-ish years longer than I've been alive, and twenty-seven-ish years longer than I was married. I just sort of started to cry a bit, instead.

Either way - we exchanged numbers. And we thanked each other a lot.

And then - I darted, as best I could with my jingly cart full of glass things, around to the side of the building where the picnic tables sort of belong to Whole Foods and sort of belong to LA Fitness and no one really knows which. I ordered a Lyft because for once I couldn't carry the necessities and the non-necessities home.

And then after Rasheed took me home, I sat at home. At Lauren's house, at least. And I paid attention to the television because that was what someone well behaved should do before somewhat-expected house guests appear.

And I didn't hear B knock at the door, and neither did the dogs, so he said *Hey*

And I said *Hello*

And all of a sudden he was there again. He was a Real Person, and he'd come all the way from Twentynine Palms on the back end of deployment, and for once I felt alright about someone else being in my space, even though none of it made sense.

I just knew I had a real friend again.

<u>now</u>

3/19/20

I guess I already had pretty strong apocalypse vibes going for me anyway, what with all the walking and the orange scrumping and the curb breakfasts, so this morning I poured the rest of my gin away and decided to get my shit together. If I was going to be hashtag-gifted a sabbatical from real life, I figured I might as well spend it doing what I'd always wanted to do and write about things. Especially while the things had a pulse and I had the time to do it.

So.

Where to begin?

I left with Sonny. We started with a walk, pausing for a couple of chicken biscuits at Quiktrip, and then we paused again for a cigarette on a different curb. For a moment I entertained the idea of actually walking to Twentynine Palms, but three days of walking wasn't going to be doable without provisions I didn't have, so I scratched that and decided we'd go downtown instead.

We didn't quite make it downtown, but we got a solid eleven miles in anyway. I played the Stoplight Game so the route was a bit of a tangle. It seemed fitting.

When I was a kid, all of our dog walks had names. It was just a thing that all three sets of grandparents did. At Grandma's, we did The Moor or we did Cardinham or we did the Well Walk. At Grandad and Liz's, there was Stithians and there was Trellissick and there was the Handkerchief Walk. And at Nan and Grandad's, we had the Figure of Eight and we had Setaside and we had Up The Track.

I liked Up The Track because the track was home to a lot of blackberry bushes, and we'd always stop at one of the so-called Tuck Shops for a snack.

But my favorite of all the walks was always Round the Graveyard. When it was dark and you shone the torch onto the trees, you'd disturb the bats, and Dad always had stories about people whose names were on the gravestones. True stories, too.

/

Back in December, after a night that was a bit like hell, I decided that the best way to not feel like hell was to take a walk. I ended up walking all the way from Aunty Kathy's house in Grove to Nan and Grandad's West Hanney, because somewhere along the way I decided that it would be nice to find Grandad's grave.

So I suppose this walk was the Grandad Walk.

Hanney was the same. Hanney was the same red-bricked, thatched-roofed, one-and-a-half laned same as it had always been. Technically the village was divided in two - East Hanney and West Hanney, although all that separated them were a couple of white signs with either one of the two names in a serif font. West Hanney was the one I was attached to, because West Hanney was the focal point of everything that was good and right and normal with what I thought about when I thought about England.

As I entered West Hanney, the village hall stood stoutly off to the right and I didn't really need to stop and look at it because, truth be told, it's a very ugly building - a very ugly building that I know like the back of my hand. The echoes of coffee mornings - the smell of tea and dish soap and Village Hall - emanated from every block of Hanney Brick. The pavement was narrow and pock-marked and wet, and my ugly foreign running shoes that looked like yachts were certainly not new-looking any more, and definitely were very much just dirty, now, what with all of the puddles.

But it was a clear day. It was a *blue skies* day, as Nan would have said, and I knew that Nan was probably very pleased about that.

The road up to the church was flooded and there was a pitiful bit of orange tape sectioning it off, as if people might not know not to drive through a flooded road. Hanney Manor still had a lot of windows, and the Vicarage still had a very neat lawn, and St James' church still jutted out from behind the giant oak trees. St. James' church wasn't a particularly quaint church, by English standards. It's all boxy and honestly a bit drab, but it was definitely my favorite of the churches nevertheless.

We'd always joked that Grandad was A Churchgoer because he was in charge of taking the giant metal key up there twice a day, every day, to unlock it in the mornings and lock it in the evenings. It was also where I'd been christened as a baby; I'd famously blown raspberries at the vicar, a story that went on to become well entrenched in Longworth family lore.

There's something about being surrounded by all that stone and lichen and script and silence that I've always rather loved. I also knew the general layout well enough to know that the newer graves had had to expand into a field out to one side, around the back, so I headed in that direction and poked around for a bit.

I wasn't entirely shocked to see names I remembered, but it was definitely - solemn. Or something. These were white-haired old ladies and men in corduroy who had fussed over me and Megan when we gatecrashed Nan's Senior Cits' coffee mornings as kids, on the hunt for the good biscuits before we shot back out to the climbing frames and the roundabouts or cycled around the car park, hollering at one another.

But none of the names were Grandad's name. Brian Longworth didn't have a little wooden square, or a marble oval. His name just wasn't there. So after a while, I had to call Megan because I couldn't find Grandad.

She said they hadn't buried him yet, and that there was a vague plan to scatter his ashes around Community Woodland. It all seemed very unceremonious.

It was even more unceremonious when, later that day, I leaned over the arm of Nan's sofa to find somewhere to put my coffee and there was a box inside a gift bag and - well, I found Grandad.

/

That day was a day that I told myself I'd give up drinking. I obviously didn't stick to it. I meant to, but I couldn't hack all the food being around and the stress of being told everyone was Concerned About Amy and, since I couldn't exactly get away from it, the alcohol kind of helped.

Earlier, Dad said that Tesco had been out of Nan's ginger wine so she'd had to make do with sherry, and she was only allowed three bottles of it at the checkout. Grandad had missed his chance to see rationing happen a second time around, I thought.

Except this time, it wasn't the Bloody Germans, and there weren't any bombs raining down on London.

Sometimes I think about the fact all of us Longworths are only here because a bomb didn't go off. The only reason they'd moved to Oxfordshire in the first place was because they'd stayed in London after the war started, and then a bomb fell through the roof of their house. And it didn't go off.

And then he'd met my Nan. And now here we all are.

/

But - anyhow. I've been brainstorming what to do with all the oranges I've been collecting from all these Phoenix Tuck Shops. The good thing about walking everywhere is that I know where all the best trees are, but it was so sad to think that all this fruit was at its ripest and no one was eating it. Dabbling in the art of preserving seemed like something I could try out, a few days ago. I'd only held off on this because making marmalade takes a lot of time, and now that I'm out of work for a bit, I guess I do have a lot of time. After all, I did hoard mason jars before I moved, because they'd make good drinking glasses and they were cheap, and the Phoenix oranges have a lot of rind, and Grandad did always rave about the virtues of a good chunky marmalade, and - well, they're the best damn oranges I've ever eaten.

And - I don't know, it would just be a pretty fine toast to Brian, wherever he ended up. And it would certainly taste good on toast.

So the end of the world as we know it is upon us, and everyone is panicking, and I'm going to start making marmalade.

The first move will, of course, be to plot out the Marmalade Walk.

<u>now</u>

3/20/20

The Marmalade Walk was a lot shorter than anticipated. Maybe a mile in total. Turns out, one good orange tree has an awful lot of oranges on it.

It only took a short amount of rifling through the tree on the corner of 10th and Campbell to yield five-ish pounds of oranges.

The first recipe called for five pounds of oranges, and the second one just said *lots*. And - well, guessy recipes were always more my style, anyway, and Geoffrey seemed to think the bag felt like it was about five pounds.

When Geoffrey approached us, I was slightly nervous that he owned the tree and he was going to tell me to stop pilfering his branches. That He Was American and It Was His Tree and so even though he wasn't using the oranges, I Oughta Get Off His Property. Or something.

Technically I wasn't on his property. I was just stealing fruit from the branches that were not on his property. And, as it happened, the man who was Geoffrey did not own the property, and he stopped a fairly safe distance away from me, and he just said that he'd tried one of these oranges before, and that it didn't taste very good.

Really? I said. *Maybe I'm weird. I just like them sour.*

Sour? He replied.

Yes. Sour.

I'm not sure if he just didn't hear me correctly or if he didn't know the word. Sour. Again I said - *sow-er*.

We got to talking while I rummaged. He pulled an orange off and ate it messily, pushing his fingers into the pulp so that little fountains of juice sprayed all over his shirt. He had tattoos all over his hands, and tattoos all over his face, too. A brown, crooked front tooth that overlapped the other one. He was saying something about a man who was working on the house up the street, and asked if I knew if he was still asking around for workers, and I said *sorry, no. I don't live on this street.*

Once I thought I was done, I handed him the bag and asked what he thought. *Does that seem like five pounds to you?*

I resisted the urge to say that back home, five pounds was called a fiver if you were talking about money. As opposed to free oranges.

Just about, he said. He was still holding the bag when he said his Gramma used to make marmalade out of oranges. Or, in his words - o*rrrn-giz*.

I retrieved the bag and shook his hand with the wrong hand because Sonny was in my right one. And I asked his name, and when he said his name was Geoffrey I smiled and said *that's my dad's name.*

It's a little-known fact that Geoffrey is my dad's legal first name. Brian changed his mind after the birth certificate was signed, so Geoffrey Peter Longworth became Pete. But legally he is still G.P. Longworth, which is funny because it was his sister who became a doctor.

Either way - I've got a lot of oranges now, and a whole day to figure out how to make something Brian might have liked. The only thing I'm missing is sugar.

<u>now</u>

3/20/20

The Sugar Walk began with me dropping Sonny off at home because I need two hands to type, and the Sugar Walk also had to begin with me writing about the Marmalade Walk, so I sacrificed Sonny in favor of having two hands.

Because I was writing about the Marmalade Walk, the Sugar Walk was inevitably longer than the Marmalade Walk, and it took me along the canal and down Central and then along Indian School. And, as it happens, my favorite Circle K is on Indian School, so I figured I'd stop in for a pack of cigarettes and to say goodbye to Billy.

Billy had become my favorite Circle K worker a little while ago, partly because he always gave Sonny meat sticks, and partly because he didn't mind it when Sonny jumped up on the counter, but mostly because he wanted to know Sonny's name and I became known as "Sonny's Mom" amongst the staff.

I also liked Billy because the license plate on his truck was *DM4 DND*.
And - well, I knew enough to know that Billy's ponytail indicated that Billy's license plate indicated that he played Dungeons and Dragons.

/

When Killian was in comm school, when we first moved to Twentynine Palms, he'd started a DND circle. It started off as four people - Killian, and Matt, and Gentry, and someone else whose name I can't remember - but after word got out that it was actually a really good time, the circle grew until it was half full of people who took it seriously, and half full of people who were really only there to drink. And then there were Wives who mostly used it as an excuse to see other Wives.

And I guess technically I was A Wife, but I played DND with the dudes so that I didn't have to be stuck chattering about Wife Things with the Wives. Mostly I used it as an excuse to drink.

/

When Billy stepped outside I noticed that he dyed his hair. It was cute, honestly. His beard was grey and the rest of his hair was sort of brown and his roots were really, really bad.

He asked if I'd be coming back. I said I would be.

Stay safe, okay? We said to one another.

Thanks. You too. Thanks.

His truck was a Tacoma, like just about half the lieutenants in the Marine Corps had, but at least his truck was electric blue. Officers didn't tend to do electric blue. Officers tended to do white and black and gun-metal grey.

before
==

11/28/18

It's 5.10am. 0510. Zero five ten.

I'm putting on my armor - Killian's sweatpants, the Bridgeport hoodie, Killian's mom's jacket. I just wrote three pages of Candace's essay. For now - I'm going to walk Sonny, listen to happy music and imagine good things.

I have to be my own shell. I have to be.

Who are we? Underneath our carapaces? We're all just fucked up lumps of flesh. That's all we are.

At last, my yolk. Those words again. I'd really just like to boil that yolk the same way everyone else seems to. I'm tired of spilling myself out.

/

The sky was so violently blue this morning.

/

I'm sitting on the step outside base legal, taking drags on a cigarette.

What is it to drag? One can dress up in drag. To *be* dragged - well, that fucking hurts. To be the one *doing* the dragging is to have power.

This cigarette is giving me power - or a kick, or courage, or something - and, at the same time, it's filling my lungs with tar. I also don't feel particularly powerful, sitting here outside the legal office, about to go into a room full of people who will all see prey. They'll know me from being around, and they might know I'm British, and they'll think *hm, she's single now, might as well hit on her.*

Well, not all of them. But some.

/

The divorce brief was weird. It smelled like a fall candle when I walked in.

Oh, it smells so festive! I commented, with a little exclamation. As in, one exclamation point.

It would have been an exclamation *mark* in England.

Either way. No one replied.

They had Nickelodeon on the TV while we waited for people to file in. They were all military, all in camis, save for a Navy guy in the khaki and black uniform - what are those clothes called? Charlies?

I recognized a couple of them from GNC. My hands were clammy and I wanted to blow my nose; I tried to wipe it, subtly, on my sleeves, but what I really needed was a good nose blow. I felt sad, down to the bone. There we were, sitting together in silence, all these people with fucked up lives - we have, all of us, exchanged tears and screams and a million cross words with the person that we once loved so much that we married them. Every one of us believed, once upon a time, that that person could give us all the happiness in the world. And now we sit together, each ready to file a stack of paperwork to become Legally Single - single on paper, single on Facebook, free to use Tinder and sniff each other's butts at will, without judgement. Or, rather - with judgement, but no legal implications.

Cross words. Killian's been doing a lot of crosswords recently.

The TV switched to Paw Patrol. It was absurd - this band of quiet, stripped individuals, sitting in this stupid office, subjected to kid's television and the legal team's sad attempts at festive decor - some limp strings of tinsel and cheap baubles on the plants.

The little clerk led us outside and across the courtyard to another room. The girl with the short hair that I recognized from GNC - she was thin and hispanic looking, with pretty eyes - started talking to a sergeant. He called her *brother*. I wasn't sure if it was deliberate.

The room was pitch dark, and they had us sit through a video that was, essentially, a slideshow with a blond lieutenant yammering in the background. I barely heard a word of it, but a few stuck out - *community property* was the phrase I wrote down.

My whole adult life is *community* fucking *property*.

I also noticed that, at the bit with the cool-off period and the graph, they'd made Louisiana purple and, in the key, while all the other colors indicated a period of time, purple just had *Louisiana???????* next to it. I wanted to ask why, but no-one else seemed to notice. Or if they did, they didn't laugh.

At the end I asked what the implications of having a deployed spouse would be. The captain said that, with a summary dissolution, if he decided to halt the process at any point, he could, but that was all. The Navy guy asked if he could still do a summary dissolution if they had kids, and if he had to go to Oregon to see a mediator. The first answer was no, and I don't remember the second one. I tuned out.

Another reason to be grateful we never had kids, I thought. *At least our divorce is easy.*

The Navy guy spoke to me, afterwards. He asked where in England I was from. And - well, at least he got the country right. I was nice enough to him, but I ran off as soon as I could. I had to figure out what the fuck to do with all these papers with all these godforsaken words on them.

I felt like I was swaying as I walked back to the PX. I didn't finish my cigarette. I saw Randall in the doorway of the barber shop and showed him the papers in my hand, with the blue words *SUMMARY DISSOLUTION* stamped right in the center of that top page.

It took him a second.

There was a Marine on the bench next to him, who probably heard our whole conversation. I told Randall that it was okay, that this whole thing was okay, and *yes I know it's divorce*, but that it was okay. And then I said I had been awake since one, and that I needed coffee. So I went to the Starbucks next door.

The snottiest of the Book Club Wives - the one who sneered when she saw that all I'd brought to drink was wine - was in line at Starbucks. And there were tigers on the holiday gift sets.

I laid the paperwork face down when Jasmine asked for my order. She noticed my ear tattoo for the first time - *I am, I am, I am*. I fumbled with my backpack to get out of explaining it. Then I sat at the window and stared into space.

This brings us to now. I came to the food court with my laptop, and I wanted to sit with the screen facing a wall so I could write without worrying about some idiot coming up behind me and reading this drivel. And, since I'm here, I got my usual breakfast because - well, fuck it, I meal prepped and forgot my food in the rush to leave.

Meal prepping is just a fancy way of saying leftovers. I can't take credit for that thought. That was a SSgt Gustafson thought. Killian mentioned it to me more than once, because it was a Funny Work Thing that I thought was funny the first time but got kind of old the second or third time.

What do I notice now? The Pepto commercial with the dancing men in pink, singing about diarrhea. Stacks of Bud Light to my right, and the sign over Walter's pizzeria. *Here's to the Heroes.*

The Navy dude thought to say *cheers* to me earlier. I just remembered that.

Cheers, then. Cheers to being back on the other side of the world from Killian, and not having someone to prod at the knot in my back from sleeping at awkward angles.

/

While I was walking up to the PX the other day, I wondered about the phrase *head over heels*. I've decided I don't like it very much - one, because it's a cliché, but also because what happens if you hit your head on the way down? Concussion? Strokes?

And if you smash it hard enough, all that sludgy brain stuff would come oozing out. And blood - lots and lots of warm, red blood.

Well, at least it makes sense. But it isn't a nice thing to imagine.

<u>now</u>

3/21/20

I was supposed to take the marmalade off the heat at 11, but I fell asleep before that.

I didn't tell B that I'd woken up a couple of hours before I spoke to him, and I neglected to mention that I'd woken up to a few fire fighters prodding at me. I guess my neighbors had been concerned that I'd fallen asleep outside the apartment, and that Sonny had been sniffing around the parking lot without a leash.

I didn't mean for it to happen. I just didn't have any structure to my day, and sleeping was hard, so I had to drink in order to sleep and - in the event of coronavirus and unemployment and not being home - that meant sleeping whenever I could.

Either way.

It's 1.43am now and I just put the marmalade in jars and I'm wondering if burnt marmalade is marketable.

My parents would probably think so, but Dad likes the taste of burnt things, and Mum just thinks everything I do is brilliant. I'll have to wait to do the taste test when it's cooled off - and, I suppose, when I make time to get some bread for toast. I figured that I would take some to Twentynine Palms. B and his friend Creg can be taste testers.

I think I recognized one of the firefighters from the other time this happened. The first thing I thought when I saw them was panic, just panic, pure panic, a white noise kind of panic. A panic about if they were going to charge me.

I asked them if they were going to charge me, and they said no. *No*, they wouldn't charge me.

I'm not sure why that was the first thing that sprung to mind, though, because they didn't charge me the first time this happened. I would have remembered that. They just parcelled me in through my front door, and I was nice to them, and then I went to sleep.

As for tonight - I got over the panic pretty quickly. They were very nice, but they tried to put my Outside Things inside when they closed the door, and then I came to my senses, and I told them *no, those stay outside*. The shoes would smell and the blanket in the bag was dusty. I wanted it outside, not in here, where everything is the way I want it.

I'm sure they were confused as to why a pretty young lady with a very pretty household had any business falling asleep on her doorstep.

<u>now</u>

3/21/20

It's early. It's still dark outside and I'm in a DH Lawrence mood. He was a grumpy old man that doesn't get celebrated enough.

Killian gave me a book of DH Lawrence's poetry before I left America. The collected poems of DH Lawrence, because he remembered how much I loved "Studies in Classic American Literature."

I don't think it was a first edition, but it was a very solid and smelly old copy. And - god, I loved that book. Now it's in Dad's attic with all the other books that wouldn't fit in my backpack when I moved back.

I never read it from start to finish. I just dipped in and out, smiling at how deliciously grumpy he was.

<u>now</u>

3/21/20

It's 10.59am, and Tom said he was going to leave at 11 to take me to the airport, so I'd better do what my parents would tell me to do and *stop faffing around.*

Get my shoes on. Brush my hair. Make Sure I Have Everything - toothbrush, cigarettes, books, ID, documents.

I cannot be separated from my documents. My passport, my green card, my marriage certificate, the pieces of the puzzle that make me a Legal Alien, for the time being.

/

I initially just wrapped up the burnt marmalade in a plastic bag, but then I thought better of it and put it in a ziplock bag. It wouldn't do to get burnt marmalade all over my things, after all. If the glass broke.

I'd really rather that B and Creg didn't think I'm a terrible cook, but they probably will. This marmalade certainly wouldn't win any prizes at a fete, and I certainly wouldn't add it to anything I'd take to a potluck.

But then again, I guess it doesn't need to.

/

I realized I was hungry before Tom showed up, so I figured I had time to shoot down to Quiktrip and grab a slice of pizza. But I barely made it a hundred feet down Highland before Tom's truck rolled up next to me, with a Tom in the driver's seat.

I explained what I was doing. He smiled. *Well, we can fix that problem,* he said.

After I pulled my backpack into the front seat and got Sonny situated in the back, we went through our options. He suggested a little deli that he liked called Cheese N Stuff.

Turkey sounded good. Rye bread also sounded good. So that's where we went.

The inside of the shop reminded me of Campus Deli, the little sandwich place in Pittsburgh that Killian worked at after I left. It was - rustic, I suppose, in that very working-class American sense. It was cramped, and charming, and wallpapered with handwritten menus and signs that described sandwiches with people names. Tom knew the owner, and the girl who worked there with him, and they chitchatted about the coronavirus, and sighed a bit, and asked about the kids, and - some other things. Like potato salad. Did I want potato salad?

No, I said. Just the sandwich was fine.

Back in the car, we sat and we opened our sandwiches, peeling the stickers from the flimsy paper wrapping. I'd never eaten marbled rye bread before, and I'm not sure why I was surprised by how soft it was, but I was surprised all the same. Tom was talking about how he'd moved to Phoenix from New York in '79 because his dad had moved here and then his dad had had a heart attack. And then he talked about his initial review of Phoenix.

Well it's fuckin' hot, but it's not bad, he said. He laughed. I was inclined to agree with him.

He also said, *It's a bitch to get sick and not be able to work.* I also agreed with that.

And I was grateful. Grateful for Tom, and the sandwich, and for the fact that Tom was going to take Sonny so that I could get back to Twentynine Palms and be with people that made more sense than other people.

<u>now</u>

3/21/20

It isn't 3/22 yet, so this still counts.

Today was weird.

I came back to Twentynine Palms, and it's pretty much the same - well, except that Stater Brothers has a new logo now, and we had to queue in order to get into the store, and there wasn't much pasta left, and the good butcher with the weird nose wasn't there.

When we pulled up to the house, Creg was sitting on a lawn chair in the front with a straw hat and some weird shoes and a ukulele, watching his uniform dry and drinking a Bud Light, and I knew I was going to be alright. The whole thing was absolutely alright.

And the view was just as good as I needed it to be.

/

Technically a mountain has to be three hundred meters high to be considered a mountain, so I don't think these are mountains, but they stretched on all the same. And the sky was all the right colors.

<u>now</u>

3/22/20

It was 5.41am when I woke up, and I probably could have gone back to sleep, but good thoughts don't tend to happen when it's light outside and I'm around other people. So I got up, and got the spluttery Mr Coffee into action.

They're typical infantry officers. They don't have anything on their walls, but they do have three coffee machines. I picked the one I knew how to use.

/

When I moved to America, the first time, I arrived at a good enough time of day for there to still be shops open. I don't know if Uber was a thing then - and even if it was, my phone wouldn't have worked yet. So I left the airport in a big, carpeted, royal blue airport shuttle. I gave the driver my new address, and we went to my new address.

5733 Holden St. I still remember the number because it's blue, purple, and double red.

Jason and Kelsey and I had been communicating via email at first, and then we moved it to Facebook, and we became Internet Friends before we were Real Friends. We'd all met on

Craigslist, and both of them were grad students - Jason did video game design at Carnegie Mellon, and Kelsey did photography at a school named after a woman. Both of them were already moved in, and the apartment was completely furnished, albeit in a Pittsburgh college student kind of way. The whole place was hand-me-downs and cheap new things, and the floors were definitely at an angle in some places, and the whole place creaked.

Either way - as soon as I walked in, I fell in love with it.

It was one of those chunky old buildings with big doorknobs and a neat little balcony set off to the side. Because I had been the first roommate Jason had found, I got to pick my room first, and so I'd picked the one that had the French doors opening out to the balcony.

Back home, I'd been worrying about where I'd put my clothes, but I hadn't known that This Was America, and that in America, built-in closets were a thing. I was pleasantly surprised to find that my room had a closet, so I had somewhere to put my clothes. I was extra surprised that I also had somewhere to sleep, because Kelsey had been kind enough to give me a bed - one of those plywood Ikea ones that sit low to the ground and have bedside tables built into the sides - and not only did I now have the luxury of Living In America, but I had the luxury of a bed that was three times the size of the bed I had come from.

I did need to get some other things, though. Bedding, for one. If I made a list, I don't still have it, but I can pretty much remember the key items - pillows, duvet, sheets, fairy lights, food.

Upon inspection of the rest of the place, I realized that they'd missed something. There wasn't a kettle in the kitchen. And what was a kitchen without a kettle? Kettles meant boiled water, which meant tea and coffee and pasta and anything else that you needed to make that involved boiled water.

So I figured I'd add one thing to our current inventory of collective items, and I'd buy a kettle for the kitchen.

Jason took me to Target, and to Giant Eagle. I would have walked, but he offered, so I took him up on his offer. It was in the Target parking lot, as we bundled my bedding and the shiny, phonebox-red kettle that I bought, that I realized that the boot of the car was called the *trunk* of the car, here. He got a real kick out of that.

Giant Eagle was the most fun part of our excursion, though. At Giant Eagle there were live lobsters in a tank that you could pick out individually, and every egg was white, and there was different packaging on things, and new foods I hadn't known about. And at the end, I was very confused because I'd totalled up what everything was going to cost but it came out to be different because, In America, we added tax at the end. No-one had told me that. It seemed like a bit of a stupid system, but I wasn't going to argue with it.

When we got back to the apartment, I took the kettle out of the box and it was broken. There was no cord on it.

Jason and Kelsey didn't know why I thought it was broken, so I had to explain to them that kettles have cords because you plug them into the wall. And then they had to explain to me that In America, kettles go on the stovetop.

And we laughed, and then I probably made my first cup of tea.

/

Sitting on the back porch - which, in Twentynine Palms, is just a slab of concrete on some sand - with my coffee and a cigarette, I am more at home than I've felt in a long time. The sun is rising, and the birds are singing, and everything feels more normal than it's felt in a long time.

You'd never know the world was ending around us.

<u>now</u>

3/22/20

It's 8.03am, and I decided to head up the road to Easy St. Easy St had been home for six delicious, disturbing months, after the divorce got underway. I had moved in with Autumn, who was also getting divorced, and we had had 22 acres of roiling, shrub-smattered desert to call our own. And the house was too big, and too dusty, and too spidery, but we loved that house. We had the best view in the world.

So it wouldn't be a trip to Twentynine Palms without tramping my way up to Easy St. I guess if I'm naming my walks now, I ought to call this walk the Walk of Shame, because at uni that's what we called walking home after you'd done something slutty. And I was pretty fucking slutty when I lived on Easy St.

But at least it was okay to be slutty. Because I was Legally Separated.

/

When I was at the airport yesterday, the man at security couldn't pronounce my legal name properly, and when he saw my birthday on my green card he said what most people in America say when they see my birthday. *Tax Day.*

Until a couple of years ago, around the time I had to start doing my taxes in America, I only ever thought of my birthday as The Day The Titanic Sank.

Dad wasn't supposed to let us see that movie, because it was a 12, and neither me or Megan were 12, but we watched it at Nan and Grandad's anyway. The rule was that when the sex bit happened, Nan would yelp and we'd have to cover our eyes with cushions.

I guess I'm thinking about that movie because it's kind of an affair movie, but mostly it's a movie about the world ending for a lot more people than just one shivery dude sliding off a random door into the ocean.

/

It's 8.22am, and I'm in the middle of the desert, and I need to pee, and the middle of the desert is a great place to pee privately, but I don't have any toilet paper.

And it's not that I didn't bring toilet paper because the Bloody Americans bought it all in the coronavirus panic. I just didn't think to bring any when I left the house.

When I was a kid, there was always a brown towel in Nan and Grandad's bathroom, and I didn't know until Emily told me when I was maybe twelve or thirteen that the brown towel was Grandad's towel for when he did a Number Two.

I had two layers on, so I took off the disposable free undershirt and used it behind a shrub.

So then I was down one item of clothing, which seems fitting for the Walk of Shame. But at least this time around, I'm wearing the right shoes and not shambling home with high heels in hand.

/

I never had to do any walks of shame when I lived at Easy St. Mostly, I'd just invite my Tinder matches over to the house and get slightly drunk and get to know them. Mostly in the Biblical sense.

Some parts were hard. Autumn got lucky, very lucky, and found herself a Jordan. Jordan had come into GNC, and they'd hit it off over a Vine reference about banana bread, and shortly after that he moved in with us. I loved them, and I still love them, and I loved seeing how happy they were, and I love seeing how happy they are, but still - it was hard. Living across the hall from two people in love, when all you're able to drag home are people who are not Your Person, is not exactly a cake walk.

Nor is it easy when your safest of friends, Alcohol, finally turns against you in a very ugly way, but you can't bear to let it go. Or when your now-ex-husband gets back from deployment and comes to pick up the stuff you boxed up for him and doesn't take most of it, so now His Stuff is Your Problem. Or knowing that your bedroom is a place where you slept with one of your now-ex-husband's Marines while you were still married, and not only are you living with the consequences of that sin but you are reminded of it every time you try to sleep. Or having to concede and come to terms with the fact that the house you live in refuses, day after day after day after day, to be clean.

But. There was so much good in that house. There were porch jams, and there were sunrises, and there were sunsets, and there was a lot, a lot, a lot of laughter.

<u>now</u>

3/24/20

I returned at exactly 12pm.

I had left for a walk, and the walk didn't have a name, and B had made me take water, but I stopped for a cigarette by the school and, sitting there, inhaling the smoke, staring at the concrete, I knew that I had to go back to the house.

I said nothing as I walked up. I just walked in, took my shoes off, arranged them under the chair, and lay down. I knew I wouldn't be able to sleep. The music was too loud. But I did know that I needed to close my eyes for a moment.

Last night I drank too much and I ended up talking about D.

/

We knew D as *Dharma Initiative Guy* at GNC. We called him that because he seemed like someone who could have been one of the scientists on the TV show "Lost."

The first time I met him was at the first ball, the comm school ball, and I was standing by the fountain when he walked up to me with his wife and said I looked like Grace Kelly.

After that, it turned out he came into GNC a lot, and since he always bought his vitamins and his herbs there, and he took a lot of vitamins and herbs, he came into GNC more than anyone else. And because he was friendly, and because he was interesting, and because he was nice to us, he became someone that would just come in just to chat, and it became known that he was allowed to come in Just To Chat when most people weren't. And that was quite a big deal after me and Autumn became Legally Single and people started to drift in without the intention of buying anything, and we had to start warding them off. Dharma Initiative Guy was the only one who was still allowed to Just Chat.

He had nicknames for us, too. It was his thing. Mine was PG. Princess Grace.

Dharma Initiative Guy was in his fifties, so he was old enough to be my dad, and - like Dad - he was only a bit taller than my height, and - unlike Dad - he was thin. And he'd been pretty highly ranked in the Marine Corps, and then he got out, and he'd stayed in Twentynine Palms, and he continued working there. And he had bad teeth, and he laughed very loudly, and he had age spots, but he took his vitamins and his herbs every day, so he took great pride in the fact that he looked younger than he actually was.

Dharma Initiative Guy was the one who took control when I wasn't sure how I was getting to Phoenix, and he said he'd take me to Phoenix, and I was grateful because I needed to leave, and I didn't let myself think about the fact he had shown me his bedroom with all the sex art on the walls.

Dharma Initiative Guy told me about how his wife and he had been estranged for fifteen years when we were on our way to Phoenix.

Dharma Initiative Guy said she'd accused him of rape.

Dharma Initiative Guy dropped me off at my hotel, and gave me a hug before he left. A very bony hug.

Dharma Initiative Guy came back. He said he just wanted to get out of Twentynine Palms and he might as well come to Phoenix to watch the baseball. He visited me at Twin Peaks and he ordered two eggs and bacon and a side of fruit, which wasn't on the menu so I had to spend a while figuring out how to put it into the system.

He said he was my Free Uber while he was in town, and he drove me home, and he took me to Target and he bought me laundry detergent and toilet paper, and I was grateful.

He started texting me. Long texts. He called them his Journal Entries. I never read them. I stopped replying to them. He sent more anyway.

He came back to Phoenix. He came back to Twin Peaks. He sat in a booth with me and Leanne and her boyfriend after my shift. When I went out to smoke, Leanne's boyfriend texted me and asked me if I thought he was hot, and I replied that that was an inappropriate question, because he had a girlfriend.

After he went back to Twentynine, Dharma Initiative Guy texted me and asked if I would *put in a good word with Leanne* for him. Leanne was twenty-one, and so I said no, because Leanne had a boyfriend and Leanne was twenty-one.

He came back to Phoenix. He bought us lunch, and over lunch I told him face-to-face that I didn't feel comfortable being a middleman for him. I told him that I didn't want to hear about sex any more. He asked if he could come back for Labor Day weekend, and I didn't know exactly when Labor Day weekend was but I vaguely knew it was a few weeks away and I couldn't really think that far ahead, so I said *sure, come back for Labor Day weekend*.

On the Tuesday before Labor Day weekend, he reminded me that Labor Day weekend was coming up, and he said he was looking forward to visiting. But I had to work all weekend, and I didn't really want to see him, so I politely told him I had to work all weekend, so he shouldn't come for Labor Day weekend.

It was Sunday night and it was five minutes before 12am, and I was in the kitchen at work, and the waitress I was closing with came in and said *Amy, there's someone waiting for you.*

It was D. He had come anyway. He was sitting there, merrily, and he called me Princess Grace. My stomach dropped. He asked if I needed a Free Uber. I didn't know what to do, so I said yes.

I went back into the kitchen. I told the others who it was, and I told them the short version of the story, and I told them I was scared, and they told me to tell him I was going out with them afterwards and that I wouldn't need a ride home.

So I went out and told him I didn't need a ride home. He seemed alright with that. He gave me a hug for a goodbye.

He leaned in and puckered his lips and planted a wet, sucky kiss on my ear.

The kiss echoed. It still echoes.

The next day, I had the day off, so I hid in my apartment and drank a lot of gin, and I was very grateful that he wouldn't know if I was home or not because there was no car in my parking spot.

He came. He knocked. He walked away. He came back. He knocked again.

He texted me. He said *Hey! I stopped by to see if you were still up to a meet up?? Hope you are feeling? :)*

I replied. I said *Hi! I just saw this. I'm having a phone down kind of day today. I'm so sorry! I just need space.*

He texted me a picture of a flower from his hike and said it was for me.

We didn't text much after that. The last time he texted me was on November 10th, and he said *Happy 244th Marine Corps Birthday! Once a part of the Marine Corps family, always a part of the Marine Corps family! :)*

I didn't reply.

/

I lay on the couch. I counted each breath.

One. White. Nothing.

Two. Green. Nothing.

Three. Red. Nothing, but Megan was born.

Four. Yellow. Nothing, but there was school.

Five. Blue. Nothing, but some gingham.

Six. Orange. Nothing, but some yelling.

Seven. Purple. Nothing, but a new house.

Eight. Orange. Nothing, but a glittery millennium T-shirt. I was scared of tornadoes.

Nine. Fuschia. Cornwall.

Ten. White grey. More Cornwall. *Kerensa.* More yelling.

Eleven. White white. More Cornwall. New school. More yelling.

Twelve. White green. School. Yelling.

Thirteen. White red. School. Yelling.

Fourteen. White yellow. School. Yelling.

Fifteen. White blue. School. Yelling. Diary.

Sixteen. White orange. School. Yelling. Grades.

Seventeen. White purple. New school. No yelling. Maarja said I was a *lone wolf.*

Eighteen. White orange. School. Grades. Good grades.

Nineteen. White fuschia. Uni. America. Grades. Good grades.

Twenty. Green grey. College. America. Killian. Okay grades.

Twenty-one. Green white. College. Finals week. I threw my drink on Killian.

Twenty-two. Green green. Wedding. Killian.

Twenty-three. Green red. Virginia. Killian.

Twenty-four. Green yellow. Twentynine. Killian.

Twenty-five. Green blue. More Twentynine. More Killian.

Twenty-six. Green orange. More Twentynine. More Killian. Less Killian.

Twenty-seven. Green purple. More Twentynine. No Killian.

I will be twenty-eight in three weeks and one day. Green orange in red weeks and white days.

/

Is Twentynine Palms home? No it is not.

Am I safe here? Yes. For now, but not forever.

/

B gave me a pep talk. He said I need to start matching my socks and giving myself structure and maybe not drinking so much. And he was right.

And then I smoked again, and he told me off for leaving the front door open because he could smell the smoke.

After I smoked, I took a shower, and I washed my hair, and I knocked an almost-empty bottle of Old Spice body wash over when I set the peppermint soap back down, so I moved the Old Spice behind the shower curtain and ending up knocking some more bottles over, and when I picked them up one of them was a bottle of 2-in-1 dog shampoo and conditioner.

When I got out of the shower, I threw the dog shampoo away.

I don't know if he knew that it was still there. But it had been there before deployment, and now things are different, and I was there to help, so - I don't know, I guess I did the thing that I thought was most helpful at the time.

<u>before</u>

11/28/18

I could really do with therapy.

What things are true about me? I have a terrible history of relying on other people for happiness. I like my own space. I don't like loud noises. I have weird sleeping patterns. I drink too much. I don't eat three square meals a day. I don't do a lot of things that people are supposed to do. The idea of driving a car makes me nauseous. I like walking. I scored 11 on the autism spectrum, which is low, but it's higher than Killian. I like being a certain weight. I also like food. I'm nice to people. I love Max. I love Sonny. I see numbers and letters as colors. One is white, two is green, three is red, four is yellow, and so on.

An opinion, for now - I'm pretty broken. I feel the fracture, resonating from somewhere very dark and bloody. I just can't find it.

Sonny is curled up on my side of the bed. I've been sleeping on Killian's side ever since he left.

It's 3.20am. That is also a true thing, for the next few seconds.

<u>now</u>

3/24/20

It's 3.33pm and B asked me to Swiffer, so I'm doing the other walk that I did yesterday, which I've dubbed the Digger Walk because there's an abandoned digger on the other side of the road to Rite Aid. And I'm not sure where the Swiffer pads are, or if they even have any, so - well, I'm walking to Rite Aid to replenish their supply of Swiffer pads.

Part of social isolation is Staying Home for anything other than Essential Reasons, and since sitting around would drive me insane and the floors need Swiffering, I'm calling this excursion Essential Reasons.

/

After Killian and I moved to Twentynine Palms, I remember us joking about the crazy people who walked along the highway.

And then I actually started walking along the highway, and ultimately the joke was on me because I was so much happier being a crazy person who walked along the highway than I was when I was A Wife, because being A Wife meant sitting around talking about Marine Wife Things with Other Wives. And I didn't like doing that very much.

/

I didn't know what synesthesia was until my Warwick interview. I don't remember how the conversation went, I just remember that I learnt about synesthesia.

I didn't get into Warwick.

I didn't get into Oxford, either. On paper I looked great, but I bombed my interview because the question was something about autobiography and authorship and I didn't know that I ought to have talked about Barthes.

I did get into Exeter, though. And Exeter was where I learnt about Barthes. And I was pretty proud of getting into Exeter, because English With Study in North America was a course that only had room for twelve people.

For the Study in North America portion, I went to Pittsburgh. And in Pittsburgh - well, that's where I met Killian.

I graduated with a decent 2:1. Instead of a literature dissertation, I did a creative writing one, and I got a high first for my analysis, which discussed Barthes, but I got a low 2:1 for the actual creative piece, which discussed Killian. It was a shame the analysis was only worth 25% of my overall grade.

At my graduation we took full advantage of the free cupcakes, and Dad drank Moo Juice - that is: milk - because it was cheaper than bottled water at the petrol station. And it was at my graduation that Killian asked my Dad for permission to marry me.

/

After a lot of paperwork and money and trains back and forth to London, I got a temporary green card and I moved back to America. I missed Killian's college graduation by a few days, but I made it to his commissioning. His Grandpa gave me a book called "How To Be An Officer's Spouse," and it was really fucking nice of him to do that. It was the first book in my second American library.

And then we got married a few days later. It wasn't a proper wedding, and none of my family were there, but all of Killian's friends showed up for it and I wore a white dress.

I had originally wanted to keep my name, but Killian was actually quite put out by that, so when I sat in front of the registrar I wrote "Amy Byrne."

/

I had to apply for a new passport around the time we got divorced, and just to keep all the names the same and for the sake of there being less faffing around with paperwork at airports, I wrote "Amy Byrne" in the box on the HM Gov website.

So I finally became part of Killian's family, by name, around the same time we split up.

/

This reminds me - I'm still supposed to get an Arizona state ID. I need one of those in order to file for unemployment.

No one ever told me that Real People - who live In America and don't have driver's licenses - need to get a state ID.

/

Amy Byrne needs a state ID.

Amy Longworth wants to write.

I want to be both people. I *need* to be both people.

But it's 5.05pm, and neither B or Creg are home, and the Digger Walk is over, and I'm supposed to Swiffer. And they've been way too good to me already. We've got a group chat going called the Homeless Encampment, and we each have a cheap garden chair to call our own, and we each have our places at the dining table, so I think I'm part of the family now. So I'm going to do the very least I can do, and I'm going to clean their floors.

<u>now</u>

3/24/20

a·poc·a·lypse
/əˈpäkəˌlips/

noun
1. *the complete final destruction of the world, as described in the biblical book of Revelation.*
2. *an event involving destruction or damage on an awesome or catastrophic scale.*

/

When I put the Swiffer pads away, I noticed the dog food.

B had come back to a cupboard full of dog food for a dog that wasn't there any more.

<u>before</u>

2/14/20

I've been spinning stories for years. That's just what I do. As a child, I would take my bike and ride it through the hedge-lined lanes of Oxfordshire, or take a tennis ball and walk with it up and down the path outside Mum's house, or buzz off ahead of the slow-footed fleet when we were out On A Walk, and I was always writing a novel in my head.

Sometimes I would write my thoughts down, but mostly I wouldn't. I'd just read books, instead, and hope that one day I'd have the time to sit and write, walk and write, sit and write, walk and write, and eventually come up with something halfway decent. Enough for my own words to be read by other people. The most gorgeous promise of them all.

And I suppose I started actually writing down my story around the time I picked up and moved halfway across the world for the promise of a home. A person. A person who was supposed to give me the family that I wanted because the one back home had mold on the walls. That's all. And he was everything to me.

And that was fine for a while, until it wasn't.

Every day was the same. And that was never exactly a bad thing, but each day became less and less interesting until there was nothing left to write about.

And then someone else walked in and - well, I had a lot to say about him.

And that's the prologue, at least.

And then one day I drank too much whiskey in LA and I left my phone unlocked and Killian found it and, when I woke up, he wasn't my husband any more. It was September 19th, and we drove home in silence, because for once in my life every word felt like it was too big for my mouth. We stopped at a truck stop outside Palm Springs and all I remember is the wind and the roaring of the highway and the sun beating down on the insufferable distance between us. And San Jacinto mountain was there, rising in front of us, and all I remember is how long he took to come back to the truck, and how I couldn't get back in because he had the keys, so I'd just stood there, ears ringing, eyes burning, not sure what to do with my hands.

After that we decided to get divorced, and we lived under the same roof for two weeks. And at long last we talked, and we laughed, because - well, at long last we were human beings again, just two human beings who didn't have to force one another's company. And we didn't tell our friends. We just coexisted as two people who finally didn't have to pretend to love each other in the way we were supposed to.

And then - he was gone. He deployed. I took our dog to the departure ceremony and everything. I ran up to him after the standing and saluting got done with, in full view of all of his Marines, who all knew the horrible thing that I did, and - it wasn't just for prosperity's sake. I really just wanted to say goodbye.

I walked home with Sonny. People offered me a ride but I walked because I needed to. I needed the air. I needed the rhythm. I needed the space.

before

semper fidelis
9/19/18

I saw him, in the whiskey mist, toward
the sliver of bathroom light. muffled creaks
under carpet. I didn't say a word.
I know everything. don't make a scene.
I was awake when the sun rose. all I
saw was red. red walls. the red room rising
& the fan, roaring. "Never Let Me Go"
lying next to the window. I cleaned my
purse of last night's scraps, just to fill the time.
Murph lurked. I sent one text - *he knows.* I ought
to clear the breadcrumbs from my phone, I thought.
a few words emerged through the white noise -
bank of hope. lucky feet. receipt. squished nose.
just put one foot in front of the other.

before

11/19/18

I went in search of eggs and cigarettes, I wrote, in my head. *Full body tinnitus. Tinder.*

Those bozos on Tinder - I didn't remember matching with them, and I was appalled at my choices. That first kid - what was his name? And the next - *Johnny*. Just another Marine, another *nameless man in green*.

Ugh.

I continued on to the gas station, regardless. There was roast beef next to the eggs - I wanted it to be ham, but I figured that beef might taste like ham, so I picked it up and figured I'd chance it.

The lady at the gas station called me "Amy," now that I think about it. She knew my name. It was so endearing, her knowing my name, and how she laughed with her beautiful eyes - they were earnest eyes, blue, and fringed with fake eyelashes.

I told her that I'd drunk too much whiskey, and she laughed again. She said, *I do too, but it's a choice!*

It had been a choice for me, too, I said, but still - ugh. I lied to her and I said I was hungry. The truth was, I wasn't hungry, I just needed to sober up.

And now - writing. Diary writing. As it turns out, beef looks like a vagina, and it doesn't taste like ham. Also, Killian is an idiot, and his birthday is tomorrow. And I still care about him enough to know he's going to need some good nudes on his birthday, because that's the only thing that American men stuck in the Middle East actually want.

I feel fat. I feel like a flesh lump, just like he says we are. Sacks of flesh. Moving around this spinning rock in the sky, at random, bumping into one another occasionally and, in our case - mostly moving past one another.

But - anyhow. I love the word *flesh*. I also love eggs, and whiskey, and writing after drinking a lot of whiskey, and I love the gas station lady, and I love Marmite for salvaging the icky gas station beef. And I love butter, for the same reason, and I wonder if loving butter makes me a proper American now. I also love sleep, and I love walking, and I love Max, and I love Sonny.

I loved M, too. I really did. The blue poem is haunting me. That morning was so perfectly *blue*. There aren't enough blue words for a sonnet. And besides -- other people wouldn't know which words look blue.

My head hurts.

I need a hug. I need someone to hold me together.

Cyan could work. But cyan is ink, and it's too loud for that morning. That morning was *periwinkle*. I want the blueness of that morning again, back when M was someone who took me on adventures and we sparkled together and laughed all the time. I want the person from the Polaroids back. I'd also just like my damn Polaroids back.

But for now - sleep.

/

I've just been on the phone with Conor for - what? An hour and nineteen minutes? A little too long. However - I just drank enough whiskey that my mind wasn't all here. I wanted to write about opposites, at one point.

Mum is thin and troubled. Dad is jovial, and ruddy-faced, like a hobbit. That's what I wrote down. It makes sense that I'm equal parts both of these people.

I also wrote - *If I were to write a poem for today, it would contain country music, and my first Payday bar. And the smell of apple pie in the air when I was close to Fuller St. And how I realized that I've begun to punctuate my life with cigarettes again.*

Where am I now? Now, in this moment? Let's take a second. Think. I want to be somewhere with cobblestones and brick, and history, and many men, and a cheap-ish cost of living.

That would be nice. But - well, now, here and now, I am drunk.

So, for now - sleep.

<u>before</u>

11/20/18

Mauve and *coral*. The shrubs are mauve. And that color in the sky - the orange-ish pink clouds first thing in the morning, when the sun comes up and everything is raw and new - is coral.

Fucking *coral. Coral.* That same word I used to describe the tacky book club wives, with their coral tank tops and their aquamarine pants and their stupid, stupid chatter about their stupid, stupid husbands.

Nevertheless - if that doesn't paint a portrait of where I'm at today, I don't know what does.

Words are interesting. I'd like a better word to describe the sunrise clouds.

I also thought about how people are like dogs. Sonny, for example, is not well trained, but I understand him. He doesn't shake or play dead or roll over when you tell him to, but he's still a good dog. And when we walk, he is an extension of my arm and I know exactly when to veer off the path, or stand over him, because I know that he'll pull my arm out of its socket to get at a stranger, or another dog. I understand Sonny perfectly, but I don't understand other dogs. They're all just doing their best, though. Just like people.

The theme here? Perspective. I like my perspective of the world. I like that when I walk, I've learnt to start paying attention to what's around me - the mauveness of the shrubs, how they change color depending on the time of day, and those coral clouds - but I know that not everyone sees the world this way. People are like dogs because - well, they're unpredictable, but when you get to know them, you understand what makes them tick. I guess the lesson here is to understand the simple fact that everyone's perspective is different.

Speaking of which - Killian has always been excellent at this. It's his birthday today, and he's stuck in Kuwait. He probably still hasn't told anyone that it's his birthday, but people have probably wished him a happy birthday because they've seen it on Facebook.

I miss him. When I said I want to hug him for a whole day, I meant it. It's not his fault we see the world differently. It's also not his fault that we see the world too differently now.

I like my world being mauve and sage and saffron. I like that I have better words for colors than *coral*. And I like that words like *smut* stick out, out of nowhere.

What is smut?

smut

/smət/

noun

1. *a small flake of soot or other dirt.*
2. *a fungal disease of grains in which parts of the ear change to black powder.*

verb

1. *mark with flakes or soot or other dirt.*
2. *infect (a plant) with smut.*

It also sounds like *slut*. It contains the word *mutt*. Like Americans, like dogs, like a genetic cocktail.

/

I've been thinking a lot about Thanksgiving too, recently. Of course, I missed twenty-two whole years of Thanksgivings, coming from England, and it took a while for my brain to wrap itself around the idea of eating roast turkey with mashed potatoes.

I didn't get it. Dad didn't get it, either. But after I got back from America, the first time, I had to explain it to him. Because after I did Thanksgiving for the first time, I did get it.

That first Thanksgiving has been playing over and over, in my head. Pennsylvania in the fall - so crisp, so alarmingly orange - and the warmth of Mrs Shiavoni, her eyes always wrinkled together from smiling so much. She had had to work that Thanksgiving, I recall, so Killian, Nick and I drove to West Virginia to be with the rest of the Shiavoni family. I barely remember them individually - except Sarah, large, funny Sarah who talked far too loudly, full of gusto for herself - but I do remember the cold back yard, and my pink sweater, and the family being so large and boisterous and welcoming the three of us as if we belonged to it.

/

Isn't the desert a place where people in the Bible went to find themselves? I need to look this up.

/

I still don't know if I need God. I never needed God. I always opted out of church; the pews were too hard, and it was always so cold.

I haven't thought about God much, in the interim, but I have come to a deep conclusion that souls must exist. I feel it, glowing, right in the deepest part of myself, somewhere full of dark blood, budding between my ribs. There *must* be souls. How else does art exist? How else do love songs exist? How else are there symphonies, and sonnets? Art is the presentation of the soul. And it is so, *so* beautiful. It is rich with other people's strangeness.

All my favorite people - all of the beautiful people that I so wish there could be more of - have beautiful souls, and they leave little pieces of it wherever they go, like those *breadcrumbs* I keep coming back to. They are feasts, these people. And, when I really think about it, I don't think there should be more of them. The beauty is in the singularity. It's too marvellous for words.

before

11/21/18

Walking Sonny this morning, there was a pair of Marines standing under the gazebo at the start of the fitness trail, surrounded by boxes. They looked like Amazon boxes, but as I got closer I realized what they were - boxes and boxes of MREs.

I made a quick decision to smile at the two green men and ask what they were doing with all of their boxes, and they said that the other green men had to run two miles carrying boxes of MREs.

I smiled again. *That sounds like hell! You guys are horrible!*

I continued on, listening to my country music. I've been on a country music kick recently. This particular playlist I always go back to is called "Tailgate Party," and it's full of songs about trucks and dashboards and cold beers and Friday nights and girls in blue jeans. Me and Nathan made a game of country music bingo inspired by it yesterday. Trevor said that if we took a shot of Bang for every time the songs mentioned any of the things on our list - and it is a fantastic list - we'd die.

This is very true.

I made a few notes. I had to walk on the sand because the groups of Marines made Sonny pull, and at this point my shin is too painful to bear much pulling. It was another beautiful morning. The desert is especially pretty at this time of year, when the light is golden and the sun is low in the sky and the shadows are long. Every shrub and rock had its own long, grey-blue shadow. The pond looked like glass, and it reminded me of a book I read when I was little, something about a glass lake with a ballerina spinning on it. It might have been Hans Christian Anderson? I need to look this up.

Later today - actually, no, very soon, so I need to stop writing - I'm going to Country Kitchen with Autumn and Jessica. I thought about the times I've been there before - first with the Wives, when they wouldn't shut up about their husbands' underwear, and then with Killian, when we were hungover and he sat next to me at the bar and he scrolled through Reddit instead of talking to me.

I was supposed to go there with M. If I'd have been there with M, we'd have sat in the corner and he'd point at things on the walls and think of facts and we'd squawk and laugh about all of the desert paraphernalia. And then go buy a fucking jackfruit or something.

Alas.

I changed tracks in my mind. I thought about going grocery shopping with Autumn later, and how I must start to cook real food for myself again. Zucchini, which in England would be called courgette. Broccoli. Ground chicken, which in England would be called minced chicken. Red peppers. Real foods. Not tins of things. I already have so many tins of things. Killian says I'm a prepper.

Anyhow. That's this morning, in a nutshell. I need to get ready now.

/

When I got home, I weighed 120.6lb, which was too much, so I took Sonny for a walk. Seven miles, maybe? It wasn't quite the whole fitness trail.

We didn't end up eating at Country Kitchen because it was closed. Instead, we went to a Mexican place in Yucca that I've already forgotten the name of.

It was such a wonderful day. I wish I had the energy to write about it.

Some things stuck out, though. Wisps of hair in the car window. Reginald the Christmas Condom being on top of the Christmas tree. How Autumn looks like my sister, with the brown hair and the milky skin and the immaculate highlighter. How beautiful both Autumn and Jessica are. How quickly I make food decisions. How quick I am when I grocery shop. How I don't like options. How remarkable it is that Jessica carts Phoebe around with such grace. How tiny Phoebe's fingernails are, how her hair looks slightly red in the sunlight, how she screwed her face up when the sun was in her eyes. How good of a baby she is. How magnificent, how miraculous it is that Phoebe is a small, pink, bald seventeen-pound mixture of Trevor and Jessica.

And, of course, the profundity of Autumn asking Phoebe to tell us our future - because she looks like a little Buddha - and how Phoebe immediately turned puce, and burst into wobbling, retching tears. *We're going to die one day, little bug. We know.*

I did mean to write a lot. I wanted to write about Jessica's comments on monogamy, and how I agree with her, even though at the back of mind I still find myself knowing that if I ever find another person, it's got to just be one person.

I thought, while I was walking Sonny, about the comment I made to Killian yesterday, about how lucky I am to have such good friends. If any good has come of this situation - and I do think there is a lot of good to be found here - it's that I see, clearer than ever, how utterly excellent my friends are. If anything, it's drawn us closer.

I'm tired. I just need to drink wine and watch "Pride and Prejudice."

I did do one good thing today, though. I did buy groceries. I bought $191 worth of vegetables and meat and Swiffer pads and wine. I also bought two packs of cigarettes so that I don't run out tomorrow. So that I won't have to walk down to Stater Brothers to see Ceann the giant register man, who has to work on Thanksgiving.

I just heard a bird singing. It's time to smoke.

/

I'm making mincemeat cookies.

I wanted to watch the movie but the whim to bake took hold. I haven't baked in months.

Who am I? I smoke too much. I drink too much wine. I bake. I write. I host events *and* I retreat away from them. I listen to country music *and* I listen to classical music. I'm a good wife *and* I think too much.

And, and, and - well, I want to have sex with other men. *And* I don't want to have sex with other men. I am loose, and I'm also not loose at all. I clam up. I'm nervous. I don't know how to let myself go. I need wine to make me feel comfortable, and then I forget. I'm fucking twenty-six years old, and I'm used to being A Wife, and I sucked myself into it for so long that I have no fucking clue how to operate outside of this. I can't read because I drink. I drink so I won't get fat.

What smart man wants a woman who doesn't have a clue about anything? I don't want a stupid man. And these Tinder men seem pretty stupid.

And this isn't good literature because - people want to relate. And who will relate to this?

I am a mollusk. I am a mollusk who must check on cookies.

/

The cookies smell like home. They're ugly, but they smell like home.

Upon further inspection - they don't taste like much. But Sonny likes them, so they're better than rice and on par with cat shit.

My shin feels better though. That's a plus.

now

stray
/strā/

verb
1. *move away aimlessly from a group or from the right course or place.*

adjective
1. *not in the right place; separated from the group or target.*
2. *PHYSICS (of a physical quantity) arising as a consequence of the laws of physics, not by deliberate design, and usually having a detrimental effect on the operation or efficiency of equipment.*

noun
1. *a stray person or thing, especially a domestic animal.*
2. *electrical phenomena interfering with radio reception.*

<u>before</u>

11/22/18

I just picked up some of the trash from the neighbor's black bin. It infuriated me, to see the two empty cans of Kickstart and the empty bottle of root beer sticking out of the top of the black bin. I detest people who don't recycle.

Like - it's so easy. Just put it in a different bin. Put it in the blue bin.

/

I have water in a pint glass. I drank almost two bottles of wine last night, and all I remember before going to bed was that I stopped watching the movie at the point Mr Collins is at the head of the table. I woke up with my alarm at six, and cuddled Sonny for a long time. The *bumps*, the *Sonbear*, the *littlest boy*, the *pony*, the *moose*.

I don't know what I'd do without him.

I weighed 116 when I checked, first thing. Mission accomplished. When I smoked, I checked my screen time - iPhones apparently now monitor your screentime - and I was appalled to find that yesterday I spent four hours and twenty-one minutes on my phone. I'd check, but I don't want to add minutes to that figure.

I didn't feel like writing when I started walking, but Sonny was tugging at some cyclists, and I looked up to see that the clouds looked like wildfire smoke. All that intense, smoky grey, with the yellow mist on the horizon. The shrubs, I noticed later, seemed particularly green today. Some were the color of rosemary bushes, some were the color of mint leaves, and some were an alarming coriander color.

Maybe other people don't like walking because they don't like being alone with their thoughts, I wrote.

And then I described Sonny. In my head.

He licks his lips when he wants to get at something. After trying to attack said thing, he turns back to look at me and he grins like he did something good, even though he almost pulled me over in the process. He's tall enough now that I can rub his ear when I dangle an arm next to him. He looks like he's a healthy weight. His eyes are amber. The fur on his back is the exact color of the desert. He has two little snaggle teeth in the front, and his back teeth are really dirty, literally brown, but I can't imagine how hard trying to clean his teeth would be. One thing I noticed recently about Sonny, though, is that he isn't a smelly dog. He smells good, even when he hasn't had a bath in months.

I also wrote - *the desert is like the tin box of trinkets that Nan used to give me.* I'm not sure if I'd remember this if there wasn't Grandad's video evidence, but I picture myself thumbing through that old Roses tin with such glee - she filled it with strings of plastic beads, toilet rolls, rustling paper, things like that.

You have to make your own entertainment. I elect to walk and make observations; other people sit in their houses and watch television. How boring it must be to be an adult that's always plugged into adult versions of Leapfrog books and games on iPads.

Other people hate the desert because they think there's nothing to do. They get bored.

Then I wrote, *maybe that's why so many marriages fail.*

Shipping containers. HITT stencil font. Igloo. Brute.

Then, the pond - there were two ducks on it, making ripples in the water. It looked like an M. Two weeks ago, I might have looked at those ducks and seen an M and thought it was a sign.

Now? Now I'm tired of signs.

Instead, I contemplated the dirt, and how it looked like an uneven spread of dinner rolls. It glistened. It was really disgusting, actually.

And finally - *Killian has an almost exclusively green name. There's that fleck of pink, like a cocktail with a glace cherry in it.*

Synesthesia will drive me mad one day. But for now, I'll just make pictures.

The bowl must be cool now. Time to make batter.

/

Thanksgiving. What a fucking portrait of men and women and our fucking gender roles. All the women in America today, waking up early to get cooking. And the men - well, I only saw men out running this morning.

I need Killian, though. I need my vegetable peeler.

Why must we peel vegetables? And why must we always perform?

I spoke to him on the phone. He said that he missed my accent when he texted me after we spoke, after he cut our conversation short with a panicky *rah*.

The whole *rah* thing had been a joke, once, because Marines say it and it also means posh people in England. Now it's just kind of embedded in the way that we talk to each other.

I missed his voice, too, though. He calms me down.

I wish he was here. Moreso, I wish that he was present when he was here. I wish that he didn't always need to be someone who had other things to do when he could have been spending time with his wife.

Sweet Caroline is playing. Of course Sweet Caroline is playing. *Let's go Pitt.* Let's go back, indeed. Back to Pittsburgh.

But we can't go back. We can only move forward, like the Toyota slogan says.

/

I am puffy. My face is pink. I really don't want to go to this Thanksgiving thing. It'll be so noisy.

But I know I need to go. I need to be around other people. The world is so goddamn noisy today. I wish I could be distracted.

What was M? A distraction. What is wine, what are cigarettes? Distractions.

What was Killian? Distracted.

I wish I could be like him. I wish I could be level headed and normal.

As I wrote that, the oven started bleeping. I took the Yorkshire puddings out, and they were perfect.

I can do this. I said I would go, so I will go.

Really, though, I'd just like to cry. I'd like to bury my face in Killian's chest and cry.

What am I thankful for this year? Walks. Writing with the others on our Zoom calls. Cigarettes. All my nice things. The animals. My friends. A soon-to-be-ex-husband who still called me on Thanksgiving after I ruined his life.

<u>now</u>

3/24/20

B called me and said the commissary was out of rotisserie chickens, so would we prefer pork or - what?

And I said I didn't really care about the meat. Did we really want to cook?

And he said *dude. Yeah. We're cooking.*

/

It was my Dad that taught me how to make a roast dinner.

At Mum's house down in Cornwall, which was technically home because she had custody of us, we didn't really have much food at the house at any given moment, and so ultimately I ended up being the one who did the cooking. If I wasn't making soup, we ate things like frozen lasagne and microwave pasta and Pot Noodles. We did have a few traditions, like how for a few years we had a thing about fish and chips on Fridays, and then at some point the Friday Thing changed to cheese and pesto toasties.

In America, cheese and pesto toasties are called grilled cheeses, with pesto.

But - anyhow. It was Dad who taught us the art of a good roast dinner. A good roast dinner was all about timing, he'd say. He'd mutter to himself while he peeled the spuds and he peeled the carrots and boiled the spuds and boiled the carrots, and he'd make exactly enough individual Yorkshire puddings in the muffin tray that everyone got at least one, and he timed everything perfectly, and the roast dinner was served when it was ready.

I watched him, when I lived with him before I moved to America, and I participated in the roast dinner process enough to vaguely figure out what the timing of all the things was.

I always preferred Big Yorkshire Puddings, though, as opposed to the individual ones that Dad made. So when I moved to America, I got the science of the roast dinner the way I wanted it down to a tee, and I stuck to it. This included Big Yorkshire Puddings.

/

We did cook.

B yelled at me from outside when I was mixing up the Yorkshire pudding batter, so I left the Yorkshire pudding batter and went outside to see what the hell he was yelling about, and - as it turned out - he'd bought a box of white Monsters, because he knew I liked white Monsters the most. He'd also bought a thing of tri-tip from the commissary, which was good because Yorkshire pudding was supposed to go with beef, anyway.

So. I did the sides. B cooked the meat. And Creg did some dishes.

The two of them were sitting at either end of the table, and I was wondering how on earth American gravy mixes work, when I introduced them to what stock was. B had been looking at a recipe, I guess, and he wanted to know what stock was, and - well, it was funny because he knew exactly what stock was in the stock market sense, and I didn't know a whole lot about the stock markets but I did, at the very least, know what stock was in the recipe sense. Stock was what Americans call broth.

I had been surprised to have found bouillon in the spice cupboard, because Americans tended not to have bouillon. But the fact they had bouillon in their spice cupboard meant that B could make stock.

I held up the jar of chicken stock that I'd used for the stuffing, and I said *this is like fifty cartons of stock in a jar.*

And then I asked why B needed stock, and he said he was going to make a sauce for the meat.

I said *in that case, you'll want this one.* I brandished the beef bouillon. *This is the cow version.*

Somehow we fuddled together a meal that mostly made sense - tri-tip, roast potatoes, Yorkshire pudding, cornbread stuffing, lumpy brown gravy, and asparagus. They washed theirs down with Bud Light, and I washed mine down with gin and La Croix, and we talked about the fact that B didn't know any of his cousins and Creg's wife was expecting a baby girl and how I saw a baby get born once and it really, really put me off the entire thing. Amongst other things.

I think all parties back home would have been quite happy with the meal we came up with. We were quite happy with it, too.

<u>now</u>

11/25/20

It was 8.43am, and it was time to do a Police Call on the cigarette butts I'd scattered around the front of the house.

I didn't know what a Police Call was until yesterday, but now I know that Police Calls are what it's called when the contractors pick up the bullet butts after the targets get shot.

Earlier, I sat and watched B make himself breakfast. He made waffles. I've never used a waffle maker, but it's basically a toastie maker, and I've used those before.

I didn't ask him to make me breakfast. But he made me a waffle anyway.

In England, you can use *waffle* as a verb. It means talking a lot.

/

After the Police Call, I took the tags and the plastic off B's chair. The last thing to come off was a sticker on the arm -

Warning.

Weight limit not to exceed 225 lbs. Exceeding weight limit can result in chair collapse and personal injury.

Made in China.

/

I haven't weighed myself in five days.

I've also stopped caring.

<u>now</u>

3/25/20

At 9.18am, I got a text reminding me that Writing Raw was happening, and was I coming?

I said *yes. I'm so sorry! I've lost track of the days.*

So I got on the call. And Jeanne had a beautiful story about a naked photoshoot she'd partaken in, back in college.

Back in May, last year, I did a naked photoshoot with my friend C. C and I had formed a sort of creative collaborative, after I'd written a poem for a photo he'd taken of a Joshua Tree. C was married, and he hadn't tried to touch me, and he had just shot his shots from a distance.

My favorite photo from the shoot was of me standing against a rock, smoking, eyes closed. I couldn't tell you where my mind was when that photo was taken. But I do know that I was peaceful.

It wasn't a sexual photo. It was just me, standing there, naked, against the rock, with my cigarette.

I got into trouble over that photoshoot. The few people who knew about it berated me for being naked in front of a man who was married.

But there wasn't anything going on between me and C. We were just friends, friends who had separate creative visions. And I don't know if C had any ulterior motives, but he never hinted that he did.

Trusting men is something I stopped doing, around that time. But I did trust C. And I still do.

I also trusted the desert, and I still do, because you can always rely on the desert for good skies, and that is one thing amongst many that I could never rely upon back in England.

/

The world was too small for me, back home. And over here, I think marriage was too small, too.

My grandparents were married for sixty-one years, I think. However many years it was, it was something over sixty. Their marriage was, quite literally, an OAP in its own right.

In England, when you're married for over sixty years, the Queen sends you a letter. And they'd received their letter, and it hung above Grandad's swivelly chair in the living room.

I always looked at my grandparents and their sixty-something years and thought that that was what happiness looked like.

But I was wrong. And I know that now. I outgrew my home and I outgrew my marriage and then, only then, did I actually grow into myself.

before

joshua tree against mist
12/7/18

we called them lorax trees, *once. against the mist, he is an aging centurion, armed with an explosion of daggers. a foghorn emerging from a cornish brume. he is a tangle of punches. and -- he is also sad, and shaggy, a wet vulture starved of flesh. he looks dejected, doleful even, like a dog after a cat swipes at it.*

each one of the bombs they play with at itx costs fifty thousand dollars, you know. fifty thousand dollars, flying through the air, shattering into a surge of flame and smoke.

he looks like the way I love people. he looks like my tinder profile, which says I am a very pleasant person *and also* go fuck yourself.

<u>now</u>

3/25/20

home
/hōm/

noun
1. *the place where one lives permanently, especially as a member of a family or household.*

/

Green cards are also called Permanent Resident cards. Which is funny, because they expire every ten years. So people with green cards are, in fact, not particularly permanent, because they have to prove over and over again that they're legally allowed to be In America. If they want to live there longer than ten years.

So I guess I'm definitely in the right place, after all.

<u>now</u>

3/25/20

It's 11.26am.

I gave this book its name before I actually knew what "Apocalypse Now" was even about.

I just Googled it. And, as it turns out, "Apocalypse Now" is a war movie that's about more than just the war.

<u>now</u>

3/25/20

It's 11.49am.

I had originally left the house with the intention of doing the Walk of Shame, but once I got to Easy St I felt more like wandering off in the opposite direction.

My ugly running shoes took me out into the sand. I stepped on a few desert weeds, and I kicked some dirt around, and I thought about how all the shades of green had different names, and how *sage* might mean one thing to me but something else to someone else.

I thought about the sign on Nan and Grandad's bathroom door. The print of the old war poster, with the man pointing at you, and the words *Your Country Needs You!* in the background.

In England, bathrooms are just called The Toilets. Everyone in America thinks they're called loos, and - well, I guess some people call them loos, but I've always just said *The Toilet*. When I got back to England in December, I had been so tickled by the fact that the toilets at Heathrow were called *TOILETS* and how, to an American, that might seem really, really weird.

Anyhow. Am I doing my bit? For the coronavirus effort? I mean - I'm certainly self isolating. I'm just self isolating outside in the middle of nowhere.

I found an old piece of sheet metal and now I'm sitting on it.

This brings us to now.

I do not have a job, at the moment, but I am happy. I am happy because I am alone in the middle of the desert. I am happy because the sun is shining. I am happy because I don't know what I weigh, and I am happy because I got to spend a portion this morning sitting on a piece of sheet metal on my own damn time in the middle of the desert and just enjoy all the sweet, sweet space.

In a way, this might be the happiest I've been in a long time because - well, I suppose I've let go of what my life was supposed to look like, and I'm just letting myself live it anyway. In my own way, with my own words.

/

a ·stray
/ə'strā/

a*dverb*

    1.   away from the correct path or direction.

2.   *into error or morally questionable behavior.*

/

Back in December, on the day I did the Grandad Walk after the day I felt like hell, I was texting B while I was walking. He sent me a picture of a river and some desert through the open end of a helicopter, and he said *the Tigris is very nice at this time of year.*

There are no words for how much it meant to me to have a friend to talk to when I was completely unravelled. And I had been completely unravelled because the world as I knew it was never going to be the same.

And now the world as we know it is never going to be the same. Everyone is saying so.

But - I don't know, but I guess my point is that there has to be good things to say about shitty situations. And, in this case, if there's one good thing to be said for the coronavirus, it's that it's a bit like The War, and The War made people slow down and stop buying too many things and just be grateful for the things they did have for the time being.

Neither me or my Grandad ever went to war. But we didn't have to go to war to feel the effects of it in our lives. And - well, we

have quite a few things in common, and our ability to withstand shitty situations with a smile on our faces is one of those things.
/

It is 3.30pm.

I have decided to go for a walk before I maybe get my act together, and maybe stop writing, and maybe call my coronavirus novel complete.

B and Creg have to work because some people are getting back from deployment at some point in the near future, so I'm going to go and make sure that when they get back to the Homeless Encampment tonight, they will get back to a house that has donuts in it.

As a former-Wife-slash-slightly-housetrained-stray, it's the very least I can do. If Amy Longworth-slash-Byrne is good at one thing, it's attempting to care about Marines. Albeit in ways that were not mentioned in "How To Be An Officer's Spouse."

<u>now</u>

3/25/20

The Jelly Donut is a donut-slash-pho-place in Twentynine Palms, and it is - without a shadow of doubt - one of the weirdest places I've ever been. Much like Twentynine Palms, it gets weirder every time I come back. And that is probably why I love it so much.

It used to be a gas station, I think. You can tell by the awning out front, and the rusty old fuel pump that was once as red as a British phone box and is mostly just covered in rust now. There are picnic benches where the cars used to be, some with yellow seats and some with grey benches. There are precisely three high top tables, too, surrounded by four bar stools covered in cracked faux leather.

At some point someone figured they'd paint the front of the building silver, so now there's patio furniture furnishing what used to be a gas station, and a brick building painted silver, and - well, that's just the outside.

On the inside, the bar with the napkins and the sugar and stuff on it has two cut-in-half slot machines for legs. There's a flashing blackboard advertising pho, and egg rolls, and shrimp rolls, and the flashing blackboard advertising the pho is on top of the display of donuts, and all the donuts are labelled with handwritten labels. Raspberry. Cream. Lemon. And so on. There's a shelf behind the register with some Buddhas and apples and teapots on it, and an orange sign on the kitchen wall that proudly announces *One Hour Service - we do you quick!*

The register guy was wearing a ball cap with the word *Fuck* embroidered on it, and he had some necklaces and a very scant moustache and a very, very long ponytail.

I told him I liked his hat before I ordered. He smiled, and he said thank you, and he asked where I was from.

England, I said.

What part? He replied.

Cornwall. He looked confused. I repeated, slower - *Corn. Wall. It's in the southwest. No one's ever heard of it.*

I didn't say that I wasn't actually from Cornwall, and that I was Actually From Oxford because Oxford is what's on my birth certificate and my passport. I also didn't say that Oxfordshire is the place that feels like somewhere I'd go back to if I ever did move back, and that in Oxfordshire there's a village called Longworth about two miles away from the villages called Hanney that I actually call home.

I said I'd just like to fill the box, please, and I'd have two of these, and two of these, and two of these, and two of these, and two of these. He started putting old fashioneds in a paper bag, at which point I realized the box was full, so I had to stop him going all the way to a dozen. He wasn't to know that I was walking home, and walking home with a box of donuts was fine, but walking home with a box of donuts and multiple paper bags of additional donuts was not fine.

The door jingled on my way out, and I sat down at one of the picnic tables.

And, as I write this, "Tennessee Whiskey" is playing on the speakers indoors.

<u>now</u>

3/28/20

There's no telling, now, when the coronavirus and the quarantine and the six-foot-rule and all of these other undetermineds are going to let up. All I know is that I'm still out of work, and my time in Twentynine Palms is coming to a close, and mostly I'd like to keep avoiding the real issues in my life with B and Creg for the foreseeable future. But that can't happen.

The donuts went down well, for a while, but donuts that ooze that much jelly aren't something that people want to eat every day. The banana bread went down better. I made banana bread because B made a comment about the brown bananas and, me being me, I decided to take it literally and embark on a banana bread mission.

We've all figured out a pretty good groove, as a household, but I've got a dog to get back to. And the dog is in Phoenix, and work is not in Phoenix, but Sonny needs his mom back.

/

After the divorce, and the shame that came with it, I fled to Phoenix, and now Phoenix is home. Phoenix is home because I called it home, because I told myself I'd make it Home, and because in my own shambly way I actually made the idea become a reality.

But - I had work. I had a reason to be there. Here. Now. Noun.

Marine Corps' wives have this phrase that they throw around. They say it over and over and over again, in their small talk and on their Facebook pages and on their household decor. They say you must Bloom Where You're Planted, over and over and over and over and over again. They say *bloom where you're planted. You must bloom where you're planted.*

Translation - *Go to a place because you followed an idea of a husband and a pile of happily ever afters there and then make it work, my friend.*

Real translation - *make the fucking best of the situation you're in.*

/

On 2/7 I wrote -

I wrenched myself out of the ground and transplanted myself somewhere new, and then wrastled with every blooming nuisance that got in my way until I blossomed.

I don't quite think I've blossomed, yet, but I'm a hell of a lot more like myself than I was before.

<u>before</u>

from: the creative writing dissertation, 2013

England was exactly the same as it had always been, but now it seemed quainter, and more endearing, and more foreign, and revoltingly familiar, all at the same time. The crowds of people in the airport had pinched faces that sagged and stuck out in strange places. This was a population of cast-offs and runts. Farm animals bespeckled the fields that thrived on either side of the motorway, giving rise to the prepubescent hills topped with small trees and small houses and small people. It was cramped, stifling. The sky was grey, and far too close.

We went straight to my grandparents' house. Dad had said they wanted to see me, but they spoke mostly to my stepmother, and they asked me no questions. When I spoke, my voice suddenly echoed with the soothing twang of a nondescript American accent, assimilated by osmosis without me realizing it. They said I sounded American now, so I sat obediently, and I shut up, and I let my thoughts drift. There was that awful image of his mother, wrapping her bones in blankets on her marriage bed.

I didn't want to think about it. I turned my attentions instead to my grandfather's peripheral chatter about The War.

Their garden had been the same as long as I could remember it - whole colonies of frogs and fish had come and gone in their neat little pond. The smiling scarecrow that Nan had positioned in front of the kitchen window to offer a bashful grin on rainy days was a bare ball of polystyrene on a ragged body now, and two of the firs had been cut down, and several additions to Grandad's collection of model airplanes in the Museum had been installed. Their world was happy and stoic, saturated occasionally by only the most minute of changes.

Grandad told me about The Bloody Americans, and their ignorance and their warped views on gun ownership, and then he paused and boasted that he had been A Very Good Shot in his day. He seemed to forget that he told us these little anecdotes quarterly, always prompted by the same topic of conversation.

Grandad didn't listen when I told him about the guns I had shot in California, or the way that the people in Pennsylvania were warm and friendly and had houses that smelled of cinnamon and fresh laundry. He didn't want to know about my America. My America may very well have just never have existed.

<u>now</u>

3/28/20

wheal - often incorrectly attributed to meaning a mine, but actually means a place of work; the names of most Cornish mines are prefixed with Wheal, such as Wheal Jane, Wheal Butson, etc.

/

porth (noun)

dialect British, South West English
1. *A small bay or cove; a river bank.*
2. *Porth (crater) Porth is a crater on the planet Mars. It is named after the town of Porth, Rhondda Cynon Taff, south Wales, United Kingdom. It is located at 21.4°N, 255.9°W and has a diameter of 9.3 km*

<u>now</u>

3/31/20

I fucked up one critical piece of marmalade making. I didn't put the date on it.

I'm back in Phoenix now. I got back yesterday morning, and Sonny was pleased to see me, and the construction men were around, and number 28 seems to be coming along.

I didn't buy bread for the marmalade. I don't really want to eat it. I can't bring myself to throw it away, but I also don't really count it as marmalade because it's burnt and - well, if it was marmalade the way it was supposed to be made, someone would have stuck a sticky label on the side of it with the date of its conception.

Dad does that with his wines, and his gins, and his beers. He sticks a label on the side and writes *elderflower wine* or *sloe gin* or *beer* with the year underneath it, and then we drink it with a roast dinner, or in front of the TV, when we're all together.

I don't know when the next time we're all going to be together is.

But I do know a few things. It's Tuesday. It's 4.49pm. It's 1649 in military time. It'll be 5 o'clock in eleven minutes, and that's as good an excuse as any to drink.

4.49 is yellow yellow fuchsia. Five is blue.

If Phoenix is going to be Home for the time being, I can rise to the occasion. As I have done.

It is 3/31. In England, that would be 31/3.

The date today is red and white. Perfect colors for a checkered jam topper. A piece of gingham fabric to cover a preserve to be sold at a village fête.

Nan can't hear very well any more. When I called her after Grandad died, she was very pleasant but she didn't really understand who I was. She knew why I was calling, and it was because Brian Was Dead, and she said *it's okay. I've got the dog. At least I've got the dog.*

Neither of us have husbands any more, but we do have dogs. And the rest of the world is a shitshow, but the dogs will keep us going.

Sonny is sitting by the pool. He won't go in the pool, because he doesn't like water, but he's sitting next to it and he's smiling nonetheless.

And Max is inside, where he should be, and we'll go back to him in a bit.

One and three is not two or seven and they are not the same colors. But there's three of us here at number twenty-seven and that's the best we're doing.

Orange is six, and orange is eight, and six is a slightly darker orange than eight, and life handed us oranges, so - well, tomorrow we'll steal some more oranges and try again to make something good out of all of this.

And Sonny will get a good walk in the meantime. Because he's one thing amongst the few that I refuse to let go of.

/

Son means *boy or man in relation to either or both of his parents.*

Sun is a noun, and it's the star we orbit.

<u>now</u>

4/2/20

The day before yesterday I was drinking by the pool, and Tiffany from number 32 saw me drinking, and she said something to the effect of *I don't want to see the fire department called on you again.*

I didn't really want to see the fire department called on me, either. Being prodded awake is no fun, and being a nuisance is also no fun, and being a liability is the least fun of all. So I decided to stop drinking, and I probably won't never drink again, but I've decided to be good for a while, and match my socks, and make sure the days have structure even when work isn't A Thing for the foreseeable future.

I really fucking like Tiffany. She's Good People, and I think the world could use more of those.

/

I do wonder about Nan. Does the decaying mind of a woman pushing ninety just become accustomed to the loneliness of being home alone with a dog she can no longer walk?

Brian's heart was fine, but his mind was not. Kay's heart is not fine, but her mind might be. Our phone conversations were very short, before I was Home. And then when I was Home, at Christmastime, we sat at the table, and we didn't really talk very much, because she couldn't hear me. And I wrote her Christmas cards for her because, in her own words, *my brain isn't working very well today.*

But it might be. It very well might be.

I think I'd prefer to think that it wasn't, though. Because the days are long, and how best do you fill your days when your husband of sixty-plus years is suddenly not alive any more? And you cannot walk your dog, any more, because you walk at a forty-five degree angle and you get short of breath all too often? And the TV only works because your dead husband wrote The Destructions on how to use it?

How do you keep going, then?

Nan has her ginger wine to look forward to, at the end of the day. At least she has that. And at least she has the dog, and a son and a daughter and another son who check in on her, over the landline, or at the table, and give her something to think about, for a bit.

She also has grandchildren, but we are in Phoenix, and London, and Bristol, and Manchester, and we can't go to her even if we could, at the moment.

And, even when I did, it was all too small. Even Sam was too small, because I'm used to Sonny, now, and a collie-dog is not the same as a big blond desert dog. And the sky behind the back garden was pretty, but it wasn't grand.

/

This Pandemic has outgrown everything I thought it might.

<u>now</u>

4/3/20

Four and three. Also fire colors.

In England, the date would be 3/4.

Jerry The Landlord pulled up next to me. I was smoking in my parking spot, and he parked in number 28's spot, and we waved at each other, and he went to go and greet the new construction men. These ones seemed nice, too, in that jovial middle-aged workman kind of way. One of them walks with his right foot out at an angle.

I'm all out of Clif bars, but I'll figure out something to offer them. Maybe a marmalade cake with the burnt marmalade.

I probably owe Jerry a cake, anyway. He's been checking in on me for months. Even before the pandemic, he'd holler out of his window at me. *Hey Amy. How are you? Stay safe, okay?*

/

It is 7.45pm. I didn't make marmalade cake. I stayed inside and read my book and was Safe. I matched my socks. I drank La Croix instead of gin. I walked Sonny.

If I had made marmalade cake, though, that would have been an excuse for a Cake Walk.

/

cake walk
/ kāk,wôk/

noun
1. *an absurdly or surprisingly easy task.*
2. *a dancing contest among African Americans in which a cake was awarded as a prize.*

I looked up the origin of the phrase earlier. As it turns out, a Cake Walk wasn't always easy. A Cake Walk was a dance, performed by slaves on their plantation grounds, and the winner would be selected by the plantation owner and presented a prize. A prize like a cake.

/

B said something else to me while I was in England. He said I have to *be the cake*.

Other people are frosting, he said. *But you have to be the cake.*

I was sitting outside a cafe near Paddington Station in London, and I had had a bit of a hellish night the night before, and I had sort of text-shrieked at B about a lot of things, and so he had called me, and I heard his voice again for the first time since we parted ways that summer. I smoked a cigarette and slurped my tea, tapping ash on the sides of the metal table and pressing my phone closer to my ear when the builders in their orange suits got louder, and I asked why frosting and cake could not be equally important. Because, I said, This Was America and In America frosting engulfs cake.

I don't remember exactly what he said after that, just that I had to be a whole person, a whole cake of my own, and we'd argued back and forth about it for a bit but ultimately I conceded. And I said *okay. I know. I'll be the cake.*

I pictured him, there, Elsewhere, where everything was dusty and sepia toned and had to be weighed down with sand bags. It had been very good of him to call.

/

When we did our baking sessions with Nan, frosting was not called frosting. Our frosting was called icing, and I think technically our icing is what Americans call glazing. It was just water and lemon juice and icing sugar, which Americans call confectioners' sugar. There wasn't anything more to it than that. It wasn't fluffy or buttery. It wasn't flavored. It was just icing.

Either way, it was our favorite part of the cake-making process. We'd spoon the icing on, and then we'd sit with our creations, decorating them with jelly diamonds and silver balls and writing icing. We'd put them in tins, and then the tins would be sealed until it was time for pudding - which is called dessert in America, and which Nan and Grandad resolutely called *Afters*.

Nan wasn't much of a Cake Person, but Dad and Grandad would select one from each of our tins and declare them scrumptious.

/

Sometimes I think about how lucky I was, or how lucky I am, to have had men in my life that were such very, very good people.

I think that's why it took me by surprise when I realized that not all men are like that.

<u>now</u>

4/4

a walk in the park
    1.   something that is very easy to do, and usually pleasant

/

Last night, I discovered a park. Sonny and I were doing a walk that I did not call the Cake Walk, because there was no point making a cake for no one, and - well, we were ambling around aimlessly, and we found a park.

It's called Steele Indian School Park. I've walked past it several times, but I always just figured that the land behind the railings must have belonged to someone, like a country club or something. But I was looking for somewhere to sit and smoke, and I noticed the gates were open, so we walked up the road and through the gates and through the parking lot, and as it so happened, this barricaded plot of land was actually an enormous, incongruous green space. A place for runners and families and picnickers and dog walkers, right here in the middle of my flat, congested, sprawling city.

I sat on the grass, near the water, under a tree that wasn't a palm tree, and - honestly, if it weren't for Camelback Mountain rising off in the distance, and the flickering American flag on its flagpole, I could very well have been in England.

So I came back this morning. I pottered along the pavements and over some hillocks and across a field that was, surprisingly, only marginally dehydrated in a few places.

And now - it is 8.59am. I am sat on a bench that is not unlike an English bench, under a tree that is not unlike an English tree, by an empty play area. The Americans would call it a Jungle Gym, but I'm not that American yet. It's a good play area, with the noughts and crosses game and a tube slide and a pretend shop window. It's just like the play area by the Village Hall, just without the wobbly motorcycle and the wobbly horse.

It took me a moment to realize that the swings have been sectioned off with yellow caution tape. As have the picnic benches. And there's a sign half in English and half in Spanish about what we Are and Are Not allowed to touch in the park. But that aside - it's almost normal. It's almost not American. It's almost not like the world isn't getting weirder by the day.

The church bells are tolling nine. A child has written the alphabet in chalk on the pavement. The alphabet will last until Wednesday, at least. That's when the next rain is forecast.

/

What do I have going for me? Now, in this moment?

I have a dog. I have a cat. I have age on my side. I have two parents I can call when I'm desperate to be home. I have a new home. The sun is shining. The sky is blue. I have a sister who turned 25 today. I have an apartment full of books. And I have an ex-husband, a very good ex-husband, who I spoke to for a bit yesterday, and who said he was proud of me for finally finishing a book.

And I have no men in my life. A-fucking-men to that.

//

So we soldiered on - out of the park, past the VA hospital, down Indian School, past the shambly motorcycle store, past the empty haberdashery, past the Circle K where Billy works, past some empty parking lots, past Mo's Pawn Shop, past the empty dance studio, past the 99 Cent Store, past the empty school field, past a few sauntering, saggy-panted men, past the empty auto shop, past the fuschias.

The only thing the future holds, for now, is a banana bread shake and some books and some dog walks. But we'll be alright. I know we'll be alright. I will hold on to this dog for dear life, and we'll get home to Max, and all of us will be alright in the end. We will be okay.

epilogue

now

noun

    1.   *the present time or moment*

acknowledgements

4/11/20

Where the fuck do I begin.

If real justice to each person were to be done, I'd probably be prattling on for half the length of this flippin' book.

Then again - can real justice to people who are Good People ever be genuinely done with words alone? No. No, it cannot. So this will suffice, for now.

I'll start with the OGs - Mum and Dad. Sue and Pete. You did good, guys. You created and raised one good daughter (spoiler alert - it wasn't me) and you ... erm, created and did an okay job with the other one, the wacko who wrote this whole thing down. All in all, you're super duper super troopers, and I love you. To the moon and back.

I guess from there, I *suppo-ose* I should move on to ol' Meg. Ah, who am I kidding - you're my little figgy pudding, you're an overall BAMF, you're a GOAT, and you're cool as all fook, mate. You'll go forth to do the best of things. To have a little sister that I a) look up to immeasurably, and b) get to call my best friend - oof, that's a powerful thing. You're a legend, my gal.

Oh, and I've gotta thank Alex for looking after you. Love ya, Alex.

From there, we have the not-Longworth sisters and brothers from other mothers - Emily, and Luke, and Emma, and Katie. You're all incredible, out there doing Good Shit in the world, and I hope that one day we can all six of us reunite with Bugs for some - hilarity, toilet talk, general pandemonium, etc. Rabble 5ever, my guys.

Then we've got the non-blood Longworths - Autumn and Alice. Whatever would a crazy pigeon lady and a Fig do without you? Significantly less halfway decent things, that's what. You're both angels.

And then - the Marin Crops *famille*. That's an extensive list that I'm almost certainly going to fuck up, but to name a few - well, lets start with wives, because this is my book and I can start wherever I damn well please. The S-6 wives (#theonlywayisS6) - Jeannie, and Simone, and Nicole, and Kari, and Rosie, and Bri, and Sam, and all of our weird little crew for the (arguably not so) great GYHM vacation of 2017. The TBS wives - there are far too many of you to name, but Candice and Brittany et al …. you're real ones. The book club wives (ft. special s/o to the Eggers family) - you gave me a genuine haven. Nykole. Amanda. Taylor. Mary. Katrina. You all are such incredible, strong women, and I love you.

And then I guess we have the devilled eggs that actually drifted into my life in meaningful ways. The GNC gangalang - Jordan, Graysen, Sammy, Ben, Davey, to name a few. My ragtag crew of others - who I shall not separate by rank and most certainly use first names for - Phillip, Dante, Paul, the Homeless Encampment. You're all Good Men - in your own very special ways. Just keep them crayons out of your diet, please.

And while we're on the subject of Marins - Killian. How utterly fortunate I am to have been married to someone as excellent as you. You'll do good wherever you go in life. Go your hardest, mate.

And then - the few from Twentynine that ended up Elsewhere, but in good ways. Candace and Cory. Shannon and David. You've been there for me at rock bottom, and you're all rockstars, and you're stuck with me. And I'm only half sorry about it.

Phoenix people - Colleen. Chris, and Ali, and Diana, and Cheyenne. The Camelback crew at OTF - Maddie, and Brooke, and Alysha and Bella and Cam and Rhian and Maggie and Ashley and Kevin. And Lauren, and Bennett. And the entire staff at Quiktrip, Dino Mart, and my favorite Circle K. All of you are the family I needed in Phoenix, where I came to self-isolate before self-isolating was a thing, and I love you immeasurably for it.

Some miscellaneous others - Kaeli. Keiran. Maarja. Alli. Kathy and Barry. Debbie. Marki. Meredith.

Post-apocalypse, though, I absolutely must thank Katie and Hope, and Kristin, and the LD team, for holding my hands through this process. And Writing Raw - Julie, and Tari, and all of our wonderful sisters - for the calls that saved me. Ricardo. Gabby. Simon. Sam.

Oh, and a sincerest of thank yous absolutely must go to every single person who bought this book when it was a sad little .pdf on my silly little website.

But the biggest of thanks must go to my grandparents. Chris and Liz. Brian and Kay. And Monica, for being the last one standing to read this. You all taught me how to love, and I will carry that with me as long as my heart still has a beat.

Printed in Great Britain
by Amazon